Heating Up
Fireside Romance Book 3

Heating Up

Fireside Romance Book 3

by Drew Hunt

jms books

FIRESIDE ROMANCE BOOK 3: HEATING UP

JMS Books LLC
10286 Staples Mill Rd. #221
Glen Allen, VA 23060
www.jms-books.com

Printed in the United States of America

ISBN: 9781478355045

For all those who asked for more Mark and Simon.

Chapter 1

"YOU FOUND US okay?" Tom asked, wrapping me in a huge
bear hug. "It's great to see you both again." He let go of me and
enveloped Mark.

"The directions you gave us were spot on," Mark mumbled
into Tom's wide shoulder.

"Come in, come in," Cliff told us when Tom had released Mark.

We were ushered into a beautifully decorated hallway. The
walls were a delicate green with darker green coving above. I
wasn't much of an interior designer, but even I could tell this
room was stunning.

"Let me take your coats, and then we'll give you the grand
tour," Tom said.

The décor and furniture in the rest of the house were just

as amazing, but still had a masculine feel.

"Your house is wonderful," Mark said once we were situated in the kitchen with cups of coffee.

"It's all his doing," Tom said as he wrapped an arm around his mate. "I wouldn't know my duck egg blue from my dusky pink."

"We don't have any pink paint," Cliff protested.

"Thank God." Tom laughed at him. "It's a pity you couldn't bring young Sam with you," he continued.

"As you know, the school year is well under way now, it's his O-level year, and his parents said he had to knuckle down for the weekend," I told them.

"I bet that went down like a dose of clap in a nunnery." Tom chuckled.

Cliff grimaced at his partner's choice of words, causing Mark and me to laugh.

"No, he wasn't best pleased." Mark sighed. "But he has to spend time with his mum, dad and baby sister."

"And his textbooks," I added, realising too late I was sounding like an old fuddy-duddy.

Tom laughed. "Poor lad."

The conversation moved on to other topics. Cliff, a high school history teacher, spent a few minutes discussing the new intake of students, the rest of us recalling how we felt on our first day in high school.

"I love the view from the guest bedroom window," I said. "All those rolling hills and the church on that little rise at the edge of the village. Just like a picture postcard."

"Yes. We're very lucky," Cliff nodded. "But apart from the local shop and post office, a pub, and the church, there isn't much else in the way of facilities. A car is pretty much an essential."

"It's a bloody pain when it snows, though. The snowplough doesn't get out this far."

"I hadn't thought of that," Mark said. "I guess there are a few advantages to living in a town."

"Are the villagers gay-friendly?" I asked.

"Not sure," Tom said. "We're not out to many…and if any more have guessed, they haven't made an issue out of it."

We all grew quiet then, but it was a comfortable quiet. My mind travelled back a couple of months to when we'd first met up on holiday. I remembered my first rather terrifying encounter with Tom. He'd overheard a conversation in the hotel reception area which had pretty much outed Mark and me. I feared he'd be a homophobe. I knew we'd come off second best in any show of strength, because the man is, well, huge. But my fears had soon proved groundless, and we had quickly begun to forge a strong friendship.

I also remembered—how could I forget—the night my awesome Mark proposed to me on that beach. Tom and Cliff had volunteered to put Sam up in their apartment for that night to allow Mark and me greater privacy. Despite my overwhelming emotions I had been uneasy about that; after all, we had only known Tom and Cliff for a week, but Mark had telephoned Paul and Helen the previous evening to ask them if it would be okay.

It had been a warm night. Mark and I took the cushions from the sofa and laid them out on the balcony to make love by the light of the moon and stars.

We slowly undressed each other, each taking a piece of clothing off the other and kissing the skin that we'd just uncovered. Once fully naked, I took both Mark's hands in mine and spent an eternity gazing into the depths of his soul through his beautiful eyes.

The slight Mediterranean breeze whispered its caress against our skin. Eventually our faces grew closer and we gave each other long, passionate, and soulful kisses.

"I need you," I whispered.

"Soon, love."

Mark and I sank down to the cushions and arranged ourselves in the classic sixty-nine position. We slowly licked around each other's manhood, teasing the heads of each other's cocks with our lips and tongues. Mark demonstrated a few techniques to me that I gratefully copied on him. Then, before either of us got too excited, Mark brought himself round to face me. We lay there kissing and stroking each other, just enjoying being close. Mark traced a path with his tongue down to my navel. He teased me there before going lower, round my dick, and, taking each of my balls into his mouth separately, treating me to a tongue bath. His humming sent indescribable pleasures through my body. Before I got too aroused, though, his tongue continued its journey to my love hole. He spent an age teasing me with his tongue. I had to put a pillow over my face a few times to stop my cries of pleasure being broadcast to our neighbours. Then, despite my protests, Mark removed his tongue.

"I'm going to open you up now, beautiful man," he whispered, squeezing some gel onto a finger.

He circled his digit around my hole, slowly adding pressure. Once he was inside, I tensed; Mark remained still until I relaxed again. He began an awesome massage of my prostate; I had to use the pillow again. He bent down and took my achingly hard prick into his mouth. He moved expertly up and down my shaft while continuing to massage with his finger.

Mark brought me to the brink several times. I had divided emotions about this; I hated him for not letting me come, but I also loved him for loving me as he was doing.

He stopped me on the brink yet again; I snarled at him to finish me off. I tried to reach my dick and do it myself, but he slapped my hand away.

"No. When you eventually come, I want it to be the best experience you've ever had."

I'd received—thanks to Mark—so many wonderful experiences that night, I wasn't sure my brain could cope with another.

In truth, he'd never teased me before enough to give me blue balls, so, impossible as it seemed, I had to lie back and let my lover do what he wanted with me.

Mark coated a second finger with the gel and inserted it. He soon had a third join the first two. When I was stretched sufficiently I begged him to enter me.

It had become part of our lovemaking for the passive partner to roll the condom onto the other's cock, so Mark handed me the foil packet.

After adding more lube to my stretched opening, Mark placed a folded pillow under the base of my spine. He lifted my legs, put my heels on his shoulders, and positioned himself for entry.

"Now, love!" I said.

Mark entered me a little more quickly than I was used to. I felt some pain, but I managed to keep smiling.

The very first time he'd penetrated me, I was a virgin, and we hadn't taken enough time to prepare. I hadn't been able to hold in my cry.

Immediately Mark had pulled out. "I can't do this," he'd said, sniffing back tears.

I'd cupped his face in my hands.

"Making love to someone should be beautiful. It can't be about causing pain."

I'd caressed his face, my heart overflowing with love for this beautiful and gentle man. "I know you would never, could never, intentionally hurt me."

"Most of the men I was forced to go with were cold, unfeeling…all they cared about was sticking it in, getting off, and pulling out." Mark had winced.

I had then kissed Mark's lips. He didn't often talk about his time on the streets; it was too painful.

"Their only concern was their own pleasure. Which, in a way, suited me because I felt dirty if I got any pleasure from what they did." Mark had returned the kiss. "At last I had a chance to show real love, and all I've done is hurt you."

I held him in my arms so tightly that night; spoke tenderly to him, trying to ease his worries, and I'd promised him he hadn't hurt me that much.

We had to wait for another evening to try again. Mark just

couldn't do it then.

So I was relieved that here, out on the balcony in Menorca, he hadn't spotted my momentary discomfort.

Due to his earlier attention to my dick, I didn't last long with him inside me. I tried all the tricks Mark had taught me to defocus, but he was too good a lover for them to work for long.

I shot load after load of cream over the pair of us. Mark held still inside me, trying to prevent his own orgasm. But he'd done such a number on me, my spasms around his dick caused him to fire off his own climax into the rubber.

Mark was right; I'd never had an orgasm like it. I just clung to him; I couldn't have moved even if the building had been on fire.

We lay spent, wrapped in each other's arms, slowly coming down from our union. The songs of the crickets and cicadas, combined with the whooshing sound of the waves from the nearby beach, accompanied our gradual return to earth. I looked up at the winking stars, too many to count. I couldn't help thinking as I gazed into the heavens, that I held the most perfect piece of that heaven in my arms.

"My beautiful Mark," I said, breaking the silence that had fallen between us, "thank you. Thank you for being my lover, my soul mate, for caring for me, for wanting to marry me. Mark, I don't have the words to tell you how deeply I love you."

He responded by giving me a gentle, tender kiss.

We made love several more times that night. Neither of us wanted the special time to end. However, exhaustion finally overcame us, and just as the first rays of light began to dawn in the eastern sky, we drifted off to sleep on the balcony, wrapped tightly in each other's embrace.

"EARTH TO SIMON, come in, Simon." Mark's voice cut in on my memories. I was back in Tom and Cliff's kitchen.

"Ah, sorry, I was a million miles away…well, a few thousand."

"Judging by your wistful smile I bet it had something to do with that Friday night in Menorca?" Cliff said.

"Yeah." I sighed.

"It was pretty romantic," Tom said.

"I had no idea Mark had such a beautiful voice," Cliff added.

"I was born with it." Mark shrugged. "I haven't had much training. Mum sent me for some singing lessons, but they didn't last long."

"We should take you to the King George. It's a really nice gay-friendly pub about twenty minutes' drive from here." Tom told us. "There'll be a pianist on tonight. You'll love it."

"They do a pretty decent bar meal, too." Cliff added.

I tensed. The last gay establishment we'd been in—the nightclub in Leeds—hadn't proved to be particularly enjoyable for me. I had been roundly ignored, even pushed out of the way, while everyone flocked around Mark.

"Okay," I said, masking my inner feelings…or so I thought.

Mark and I went upstairs to get ready. We were told to remain casual; it wasn't a dressy place.

"Will you be all right?" Mark asked me.

I smiled and tried to loosen up. It would be fine.

Mark gave me a hug.

"What did I do to land a great man like you? Not to mention one who's handsome, sexy, funny—"

He kissed me on the nose. "Silly. It's just a pub, not a nightclub, but if you feel uncomfortable, I'll ask them to bring us back."

"Have I told you today how much I love you?" I asked.

"Erm…let me think." Mark creased his brow in mock concentration.

I tapped his arm. He laughed.

THE KING GEORGE was an old-fashioned looking place, not

exactly spit and sawdust, but at least it hadn't been turned into one of those soulless chain pubs, nor thankfully one of those ghastly trendy wine bars. No, the George, as it was affectionately called, was a cosy, warm, and welcoming place.

"What's your poison, gentlemen?" the landlord asked.

Tom got our drink orders from us.

"Say, Gary," Tom asked, "is Tim playing tonight?"

"He should be in around half eight as usual."

Tom turned to me and Mark and told us Tim was the pianist he'd talked of earlier. "He just plays a few numbers, and the regulars join in if they know the words."

"And also if they don't," Gary added.

"Can we have some menus, please, Gary?" Cliff asked.

"Sure." Gary ducked under the bar and came up holding the promised menus. "There's a few specials on the blackboard, too."

We got our drinks and settled down at a table in one of the corners.

"It's nice and quiet here," Mark said, having a good look round.

"It'll liven up later," Tom said, taking a pull on his pint of Diet Coke.

"Been coming here long?" I asked.

"About five years, isn't it, love?" Tom leaned over to his right and kissed Cliff's cheek.

I was surprised to see Tom display such affection in public, but Cliff didn't seem to mind.

"Don't look so shocked, Simon," Tom said. "It's about eighty percent gay in here. They don't mind kissing and cuddling. Though I think they'd draw the line at all-out sex on top of the bar."

Mark laughed, Cliff smiled, and I felt shocked.

"Honestly," Cliff said to me. "Take Mark's hand."

We reached for each other, neither sure it was a good idea. However, no one started shouting.

Tom smiled over at us. "Liberating, isn't it?"

"I wish we could do this in the pub at home." Mark sighed.

"I don't think Ron would mind. I've always had my suspicions about him," I said.

"So you've been making eyes at the landlord of the Mucky Duck?" Mark raised an eyebrow at me.

"You have to admit, he's a bit tasty."

Mark laughed.

"But he doesn't hold a candle to you." I squeezed his hand.

In a rare moment of bravery I leant over and kissed Mark full on the lips. He was shocked, and so was I, come to think of it.

"Well done," Cliff told us.

I felt my cheeks grow warm and, looking over at Mark, saw that he, too, was blushing.

We decided what we wanted to eat and I put in our order when I went up to the bar for the next round of drinks.

On my return I heard Cliff say, "It's so sad, though. Doug was such a great guy."

"Have I missed something?" I asked.

"We were just talking about Tim the pianist. He's such a sweetie," Cliff said. "Doug, his lover for over twenty years, was one of the first people we knew who died of an AIDS-related illness. By some miracle Tim didn't get it, but he took Doug's death very badly. Doug used to sing while Tim played. We only saw them a few times before Doug grew too ill to sing anymore."

The conversation among the four of us carried on flowing. It was as if we'd known each other all our lives. We just got on so well together.

"So, Simon," Cliff said, "have you gotten used to wearing a wedding ring yet?"

I looked down at the gold band on the ring finger of my left hand. "It's wonderful. I often find myself rubbing it between the fingers of my right hand. It's like I've always got a piece of Mark with me." I leant over and kissed him again. I could get used to this, I thought.

"It was a bit weird at first for me. I'd never worn any type of ring before," Mark said.

"Did you two ever think about buying rings for each other?" I asked.

"Not really," Tom said. "But seeing you two with them makes me think that it wouldn't be such a bad idea."

"I hadn't really thought about it much myself either," Cliff admitted. "But I might be talked into it." He leaned over and gave Tom another kiss.

Our food arrived. "You two old romantics at it again?" the server said.

"Yeah, Tina, got to keep my man well stocked with loving," Tom told her.

"Haven't seen you two here before," she said, smiling at Mark and me.

"We're visiting Tom and Cliff for the weekend," Mark said, still holding my hand.

"Aw, another happy couple."

"Absolutely," Mark said, lifting my hand and kissing my wedding ring.

This caused me to blush. However, it didn't stop me from pulling Mark toward me and kissing him on the lips.

"Go for it, you two." The comment came from another male couple that had just approached our table.

This, of course, did nothing to diminish the heat on my cheeks.

"Keith, you old sod. Thought we'd see you two in here tonight," Tom said to the slightly more thick-set of the pair.

"We decided to come and check out any new cute guys who might show up," Keith said, looking over at Mark and licking his lips. "And you are certainly cute. Where have you been all my life, babycakes?"

My hackles began to rise. Mark spotted this and laid a hand on my shoulder.

"These are our very good friends, Simon and Mark," Tom said. "And they're off limits. So you two can put your claws away right now," he said firmly.

Al and Keith took the table next to us.

We began to tuck into our food. It was good and plentiful.

"Haven't seen you two in here for a couple of weeks," Al said, speaking for the first time.

"Cliff's been busy, what with the start of school and everything," Tom said.

"Ah, right. You two always were homebodies."

"And proud of it," Cliff said.

"So who are your friends?" Al asked.

I wiped my mouth on the paper napkin. "I'm Simon, and this is my one and only, Mark."

"We met Simon and Mark in Menorca last August," Tom told them, no doubt anticipating their next question.

"I remember you saying you wanted a quiet holiday, that figures," Keith said.

"Yes, and we enjoyed it. Thanks in no small part to Simon and Mark here, and their young friend Sam," Cliff added.

"Who's Sam?" Keith asked, no doubt sensing a bit of gossip.

"A neighbour," I said, not adding any further information.

"Right. So long as you all had a good time," Keith said.

"We did," Mark told them.

We continued our meal while Al and Keith asked the occasional question.

Some time later, a chubby man who was probably in his mid forties, with thick-rimmed spectacles and a thinning mop of black hair, walked towards our table. He was smiling, but it didn't reach his eyes.

"Hello strangers," the man said as he pulled up a chair to our table.

"Hi, Tim," Cliff said as he put an arm around the man's shoulders and gave him a hug. "How have you been keeping?"

"Oh, you know," he said quietly.

"With the new school year and everything, I haven't felt much like coming out of a Friday evening," Cliff said. Looking at us, then back at Tim, Cliff continued, "these are a couple of guys we met on holiday this summer. Tim, please meet Simon and Mark."

We all shook hands.

"Tim is our pianist for tonight," Tom told us. "I hope you'll give us a few good numbers."

"I'll do my best. I can't deviate much from the usual, though. This crowd is pretty set in its ways." He gave a weak smile. "Well, I'd better go and see if the old Joanna is still in tune. See you later."

Tim walked off towards the back of the pub and stepped up to a baby grand on a slightly raised platform. He began to play softly, the crowd gradually growing quiet.

Tim was a good pianist. He played many songs I'd listened to for years, and they brought back happy memories of times spent at Gran's house listening to her cast recordings of movie musicals and the like. Mark and I loved many of the old show tunes, which I realised made us stereotypically gay.

Show tunes seemed to form the majority of Tim's repertoire.

When Tim took a break, Mark got up and asked us if we wanted another drink. "Should I get one for Tim?" Mark asked.

"That's kind of you; he'll have a tomato juice, but no Worcester sauce."

After exchanging words with a few of the regulars, Tim came over to our table.

"Mark's gone up to get you a tomato juice," I told him.

"Thank you."

"How long have you played the piano?" I asked.

"Since high school. I hated games and PE. I was always the last one to be picked when teams were chosen. 'Oh, sir, we had him on our team last time.'" Tim gave a pained grimace. "So eventually the games teacher let me off. It so happened that the head of music at the school had a free period during my games lesson, and I'd always had a hankering to play the piano, but he didn't have the time during my normal music lesson.

"To cut a long story short, Mr Jones taught me to play while the rest of my class were knee deep in mud on the playing fields."

"Do you play as a full-time job?"

"Oh, no, it's always been a sideline. I'm a solicitor's clerk during the day."

"Mark has a great voice," Cliff chipped in. "He hasn't had a great deal of training, but he sang for us when we were on holiday, and he brought the house down. Would you let him sing a couple of numbers with you?"

Tim dropped his gaze and grew quiet. "I haven't accompanied anyone since my Dougie was taken, I don't know if I could…"

"I know it's painful, but it might help you move on," Cliff said gently while holding Tim's hand.

Tim let out a breath, lifted his head, squared his shoulders, and said, "if Mark's agreeable…we could try a couple of numbers. What register is he?"

"Baritone," I said.

Tim swallowed. "Same as my Dougie."

"Give it a try, mate. If it doesn't work out, I'm sure everyone'll understand," Tom told Tim.

I wasn't sure if Mark would want to sing in public. He, like me, didn't like drawing too much attention to himself. Mark still hadn't come back from the bar. I got up and told the others I'd give him a hand. I thought we'd stand a better chance of hearing Mark sing if I had a quiet word with him first.

"Hi, love," Mark said as we queued.

I had a moment of panic hearing Mark say that in public, then I realised where we were, and relaxed again. I'd grown so used to having to hide my relationship with Mark from general view that it came as second nature to me now.

Smiling, I said, "I thought I'd come and give you a hand with the drinks."

"Thanks."

"Also," my smile faltered, "would you think about getting up and singing a couple of numbers with Tim?" I held up a hand to forestall Mark's objection. "He, Tim I mean, said he hasn't accompanied anyone since Doug, and we, that's me, Cliff and Tom, think it might help him, Tim, I mean, get back into things." I shut my mouth, realising I was babbling. But it seemed I was on a roll and couldn't help myself. "And I want everyone here to know what a beautiful voice my man has."

Mark smiled but shook his head. "I haven't sung in public much, and I'm not sure I know all the words to many songs."

"Please, think about it. Have a word with Tim and...please?" I brought out my best puppy eyes.

Mark smiled again, sighed, and said, "all right, I'll think about it."

I gave him one of my winning smiles. I knew he'd do it. Mark had reached the front of the queue by this point, so he gave his drink order, and I helped carry the glasses back to the table.

"Erm, Mark," Tim began. "The others here say you sing a bit. They've been twisting my arm to accompany you."

"Yeah...Simon said. But I don't know if I can remember all the words to many of the songs you play."

"Don't worry about that. Can you read music?"

"Well, a bit, it's a while since I tried."

"You should be able to read the words without any difficulty anyway. I've got the sheet music for most of the popular shows in the piano stool. I don't use them much myself as I could probably play most of them in my sleep. So you could read the words straight from the page.

"Look, I'm sorry, I'd hate to put any pressure on you. I'm a bit nervous about it myself if the truth be known."

"You'll be fine...both of you," Tom encouraged.

"Maybe," Tim and Mark said at the same time, causing them both to smile.

"I'll come up and see what I can find, then," Mark conceded.

I gave my man a winning smile. "You'll knock 'em dead. But please don't sing 'Younger Than Springtime'."

Mark had sung the ballad from South Pacific to me back in Menorca just before he'd taken me onto the beach and asked me to marry him. The words, the romantic setting, and the wedding ring had all combined to leave me an emotional wreck, and I wasn't eager to disgrace myself in public like that again.

Mark smiled and shook his head. "I promise."

Tim pointed out that, as he and Mark hadn't worked together before, things might not be as polished as he would have liked. We sent them up to the piano to look through a few numbers.

A short while later Tim started playing and Mark's beautiful voice joined in. I couldn't hide the pride I felt at seeing Mark up there entertaining the regulars.

At the end of the first number, "Summertime from Porgy and Bess," Tim and Mark got a polite round of applause. I could tell Mark was nervous, so I gave him a warm smile and a double thumbs up.

They performed a couple more songs, then they did "Can't Help Lovin' Dat Man" from *Show Boat*.

Once they'd completed their set, the pub broke out into enthusiastic clapping. I was one of the first to get up on stage to offer my congratulations.

"Dougie would have been so proud of you," a rapidly blinking Tim told Mark, who nodded his thanks.

"You were fantastic!" I told Mark.

"Thanks. I wobbled a bit at the beginning, but I got more confident as we went on."

"I'm really proud of you."

Gary came over to congratulate Mark. "It's ages since Tim had a musical partner. It makes a big difference."

"I think it was too soon for him."

We looked over at Tim, who was being swallowed up in one of Tom's bear hugs.

"Doug was a fantastic bloke, one of the few people I was proud to call a friend, but Tim has to move on," Gary said.

Cliff led Tim back to us. The man seemed to be a lot more composed, even managing a small smile.

"Mark, thank you." Tim took Mark's hand and gave it a squeeze.

"I enjoyed myself," Mark replied.

"You were excellent. Like I said, my Dougie would have

been proud." The mention of his late partner's name caused Tim's face to fall. "Sorry."

"It's okay," Mark consoled. "I've only known Simon here for just over a year, but if I lost him, I'd..." Mark shuddered.

The pub began to empty. Gary came back with Tim's fee, then tried to hand some money to Mark.

"I don't want anything. I only did it this once to help Tim."

"No, Gary's right," Tim said. "You made a difference this evening."

Turning to the landlord, Mark said, "Would you put whatever you were going to give me in the AIDS research box on the bar?"

"Bless you," Tim said.

"YOU DON'T WANT to make a regular thing of it?" Tom asked from the driver's seat as he drove us back to his and Cliff's house.

"Nah." Mark shook his head. "I like singing, but I don't want to make it a permanent part of my life. Besides, I don't know where I'd be able to sing that sort of thing back home."

"You could always come back and sing at the George. It isn't too much of a drive, is it?" Cliff asked.

"It isn't that far, no," I admitted.

"Well, perhaps we could do it again in a few weeks," Mark said. "I'm not all that comfortable about singing in public."

"If you decide to sing again, you're very welcome to stay at our place," Tom told us.

"Thanks." Mark yawned.

"We'll bear it in mind," I said, wrapping an arm around my man and giving him a half hug. Through a yawn of my own I said, "I think we'll go straight to bed when we get in if you two don't mind."

"Of course we don't mind," Tom said. "I was up at five this morning for my post round, so I'm pretty knackered myself."

Chapter 2

THE MOVEMENT OF the bed woke me the next morning. I opened my eyes just enough to see Mark getting back under the covers.

"Did I wake you?" his sleepy voice asked.

"No." I yawned. "I think I was about due to wake anyway. What time is it?"

I heard Mark fumbling with something on his side of the bed. "Just after eight."

"Is the bathroom free?"

"There was no one waiting when I came out." Mark yawned, rubbed his bristly chin, and farted. "Sorry," he chuckled. "Couldn't help it."

I shook my head at Mark trying to fan the smell my way. I got out of bed and went in search of my bag to get out a clean pair of briefs. Before I met Mark I would always sleep in boxer shorts, but we soon discovered it was far nicer if we both slept in the nude.

WHEN I EMERGED from the bathroom, I spotted Cliff coming out of the master bedroom.

"Sleep okay?" he asked.

"Yes, thanks." I nodded.

Cliff smiled. "I'll start breakfast in a quarter of an hour if that's okay?"

"Thanks," I said as I re-entered the guestroom.

"Simon?" Mark asked, sitting on the side of the bed, his back to me. He hadn't started to dress.

There was something in his tone that made me pause, sweater halfway down my chest. "Yeah?"

"I want to tell Cliff and Tom…about my past."

"Are you sure?"

"No one, apart from you, knows the whole story." In a quieter voice he continued, "though there's a small part that you don't know either. Telling them might help me deal with it better, too."

I pulled my jumper down the rest of the way and reached out to place a supportive hand on Mark's shoulder.

"Thanks," Mark said, turning to look up at me.

"WILL A TRADITIONAL fried English breakfast be okay for you?" Cliff asked when Mark and I had made it downstairs. "The human dustbin over there insists on it at the weekend." He pointed at Tom, who was sitting at the kitchen table looking hungry.

"I need building up at the weekends," Tom defended. "I don't have time for much in the mornings during the week."

I told Cliff a fried breakfast would be fine.

❖

"WANT TO HAVE a look around York today?" Tom asked us once the breakfast dishes had been cleared away.

"It's been years since I last visited York," I said.

"Before we leave…" Mark started to say, then bit his lip.

I reached over and gave his hand a squeeze, encouraging him to continue.

"Could we go into the living room? I want to tell you both something."

Tom and Cliff were surprised at Mark's request.

Once we were situated in the front room, cups of coffee politely declined, Mark began. "You remember when we first met in Menorca?"

Cliff nodded.

"Well," Mark swallowed.

I thought maybe we should have accepted the offer of coffee after all.

"Cliff, you told us how you and Tom got together. You were going through a painful period in your life."

Cliff had been bullied at school because of his size and lack of athletic ability.

"Well, you remember us telling you that Simon and I bumped into each other in the street?"

Both Tom and Cliff indicated they remembered the conversation.

Mark started to pick at the pocket of his jeans.

I put a hand over his and gave it a squeeze. "It's okay, love."

Clearing his throat, Mark continued. "Simon and I did bump into each other in the street, but it's a lot more involved than that." He paused for a deep breath. "My mum died when I was eighteen. One of the last things she asked me to do was to take care of Dad after she'd gone. Dad and I never got on well." Turning to me, he said, "I'm sorry…this is the part you don't know. Mum and Dad had me late in their lives. I had an older brother, Justin. He and Dad would play football together, go fishing, watch sport on the television, that sort of thing. The two of them were inseparable. Justin was the apple of my dad's eye.

"When he was ten Justin started to become ill. The doctors soon found out the cause…he had leukaemia. They tried to get a bone marrow donor, but they couldn't find a match.

"Justin steadily grew weaker and weaker…and eventually died."

"I'm sorry." I said, rubbing circles on his back.

"I never knew my brother, he died before I was born. I think I only ever saw one photo of him. Dad burnt most of them not long after Justin's funeral. Dad blamed himself, and withdrew almost totally from Mum.

"Dad was pretty angry with Mum when he found out she was pregnant with me. He wanted her to get an abortion. Mum wouldn't. She rarely stood up to dad, but she did on this occasion. Which is a good thing because abortions weren't legal back then…she'd have had to go and have it done by a back-street abortionist."

"Yes," I said quietly, unable to contemplate the thought of never having known Mark.

"So I was born. Dad hardly ever had anything to do with me. I guess he thought, if he didn't love me, if I died, it would hurt him less."

I rubbed his back again.

Mark then told Tom and Cliff how he'd been kicked out of his house for being gay, that he'd bought a bus ticket and ended up in Littleborough. He then went on to tell how he'd been tricked into owing a man—Jake—a favour and how he'd had to pay back his debt by selling himself on the street.

As I'd expected, all I saw was love and concern reflected in Cliff's and Tom's faces.

Mark glanced at me when he got to the point of the story where I appeared in it. I nodded for him to continue.

"One day I was standing in my usual spot when Simon came along. There was something in Simon's eyes that told me I could trust him." He smiled at me. "So I agreed to go home with him.

"Simon was one of the few men who showed genuine concern for my wellbeing. I just knew he was a good man.

"It was raining when I left his house that night. I only had on a T-shirt. Simon insisted I take a warm sweater and a raincoat. No one had offered to do anything like that before. He even fed me. I hadn't eaten much that day. My pimp used to take most of what I earned.

"I saw Simon every couple of weeks or so for a few months." Mark sighed. "One night at Jake's place, I heard an explosion. I ran into the next room to find out what had happened. It was a total disaster area in there. I was pretty sure Jake was dead, but the other two men in there with him were screaming something horrible. I gave what help I could, but I got some acid on my hands. I don't know why they were mucking about with acid. Someone later thought Jake was trying to manufacture drugs, I don't know, I can't imagine why someone would need acid to make drugs. Jake died, so we'll never know the real reason. My hands hurt like hell, though. Someone must have called the police, and soon after the explosion they arrived, they called for an ambulance, and I was admitted to hospital. They didn't really need to keep me in long, but I had nowhere to go. I even thought I'd have to go back to Newcastle, but I doubted if my dad would have had me back."

I squeezed Mark's hand, silently congratulating him for getting through the hard part.

"I woke up one day in the hospital and Simon was sitting by my bed. He listened to my tale of woe and insisted he was going to look after me. I couldn't do anything for myself at all. I even needed help in the bathroom."

Tom laughed.

"I know." Mark smiled. "But Simon here was absolutely great about it all. He looked after me so well, I was beginning to fall in love with him. But I couldn't tell him because, well, I wasn't much of a catch, no money, no home and being a prostitute. I also had to be certain of my feelings. I knew he deserved someone who genuinely loved him for the kind person he was, not for the things he could provide. So I waited until I was sure I was truly in love with him."

I smiled, thinking back to those times, which had been just as much a struggle for me as for Mark.

"On Christmas morning I couldn't hold in my feelings any longer, so I told Simon that I loved him. The most wonderful part of it was, he said he loved me, too." Mark turned to face me. "Thank you. Heck," he sniffed, "that sounds so inadequate."

"You're welcome," I croaked out through a tightened throat. After saying them, my words sounded just as inadequate as Mark thought his were.

Tom and Cliff came over to pat us on the back. They thanked Mark for trusting them with his secret.

We sat quietly for a while, Tom and Cliff giving Mark and me the space we needed.

Eventually I broke the silence. "I'm sorry, but I don't fancy trekking into York."

Mark squeezed my hand. Turning to Cliff he asked, "Do you mind?"

"Don't be silly, of course we don't mind," Cliff said. "Besides, the weather looks to be closing in," he said, getting up and looking out of the window.

We spent the rest of the day in each other's company, reliving the happy events of our shared Menorcan holiday. Cliff, much to Tom's consternation, suggested getting out the photos of their previous trips abroad.

"They don't want to look at pictures of us standing in front of the Eiffel Tower, Brandenburg Gate, and the Leaning Tower of Pizza."

"Pisa," Cliff corrected, smiling at his man.

I suspected Tom had made the mistake deliberately.

"We'd love to look at your holiday pictures," Mark said.

So Cliff got them out. Most were of Tom; I assumed Cliff was operating the camera. Though there were a few of them both together.

"At least you haven't suffered the indignity of having your baby photos being shown around," I said to Tom, remembering when my mum had shown Mark my baby photographs.

Mark laughed. "Aw, you were a cute little baby," he said, pinching my cheeks.

The others laughed.

"I guess I can be thankful for small mercies, then," Tom replied.

"I've still got that album your mother lent me," Cliff said.

"Don't you bloody dare!" Tom exclaimed.

ABOUT FOUR O'CLOCK, Tom admitted he had to get out of the house.

"He gets cabin fever if he's cooped up too long," Cliff explained.

"It looks like it's brightened up out there; do you two want to come for a walk with us?" Tom asked Mark and me.

Mark looked at me, and I nodded.

"Thanks. A walk will do us good," Mark said.

As we walked along a footpath that wound its way through a field, I said, "It looks so bare now the crop has been harvested."

"You should see it in the spring, or better still, during the summer months."

"Why don't we walk up Halter's Hill and watch the sunset?" Tom suggested.

There was general agreement, so at the next intersection in the network of footpaths that seemed to span the area, we veered to our right. The path soon became steeper as we ascended the hill.

"I always think they are such stupid creatures," I said, pointing to a field with some sheep lazily grazing in it.

"They aren't the brightest of animals," Cliff admitted. "But I quite like them, especially when they're still lambs and are running around."

Spotting a stile in the fence ahead of us, I quickened my step and was the first over it. Mark was next. I stuck out my hand to guide him across. He took my hand in preference to the fencepost.

"You planned that little act of chivalry." Mark smiled at me.

"I cannot tell a lie," I said, giving a slight bow. "If there had been a puddle, and if I were wearing a cloak, I'd have lain it over the puddle to aid your passage."

"You daft bugger!" Tom said as he crossed over the stile. Though I noticed he, too, helped his man get over the fence.

We laughed at our silliness.

Eventually Tom stopped climbing and looked towards the setting sun. "I think this is as good a place as any."

We agreed.

Tom sat on the ground, his back against a boulder. Cliff settled into the space between Tom's legs, resting his back against Tom's chest. Tom put his chin on top of Cliff's head and wrapped his arms around the smaller man.

The size differential between Mark and me wasn't as great. However, I spotted another rock close by, so sat on it and invited Mark to sit on the ground between my legs. We then adopted the same cuddling position as the other two.

The kaleidoscope of yellows and oranges as the sun slowly dipped below the horizon was magnificent. I kissed the top of Mark's head, pleased I was able to share such a wonderful moment with him.

"We better get down while it's still light," Cliff said.

We wended our way back to the village, walking hand in hand when the footpaths permitted.

"Why don't we stop off at the Coach and Horses for a pint before dinner?" Tom suggested.

We all agreed, so Tom led the way to the local pub.

Cliff had put a casserole in the oven on low before we'd set off, so there was no need to hurry back.

We made it to the pub just as the last of the daylight faded into darkness. As we stepped inside from the rapidly cooling outdoors we welcomed the warm, if smoky, atmosphere with gratitude. Alas, it would be many years before smoking in public places would be made illegal.

It being a Saturday night, the place was busy. We did manage to snatch some seats close to the snooker table. Our location did come with a few unexpected fringe benefits, however. The sight of the players' bums as they bent over to take their shots wasn't exactly unappealing. Mark gave me a knowing grin once he'd spotted what I was up to.

As time passed, the place became increasingly crowded, noisy, and smoke-filled. Once our glasses were empty, we decided to make our way back to Tom and Cliff's place.

"THIS MUTTON STEW is really tasty," Tom said.

Cliff shook his head. "In polite circles it's called a lamb carbonnade."

Tom looked at Mark and me before turning to Cliff. "It's only Simon and Mark." He then shovelled in another huge forkful of stew.

Cliff smiled and shook his head once again.

"Any more bread?" Tom asked, dipping the last piece in the gravy on his plate.

"You've had four slices already." Cliff stood and reached for the bread crock. To Mark and me he said, "Our food bills are out of this world."

"I'm a growing boy," Tom protested.

"Whatever you say." Cliff patted Tom's shoulder and laid another couple of slices next to his plate.

"Thanks." Tom smiled at his partner.

"Do you do much of the cooking, Tom?" Mark asked.

"Because I'm home way before Cliff, I usually get the tea underway."

"Yeah, it's the same for me," Mark admitted.

"You'd have thought with him preparing food all day, he'd have seen enough of the stuff without starting up again at home," I said.

"I don't mind," Mark admitted. "Besides, sometimes I bring home something from the café if there's anything good left over."

Mark and I insisted on doing the washing up. Cliff was adamant that guests didn't do the washing up. Mark told him we weren't guests, we were friends.

"And as you've put so much effort into preparing the food," Mark told him, "we can't sit by and watch you clean up, too."

Cliff caved, but insisted on helping.

"I might as well put the stuff away, as I know where everything goes."

We couldn't argue with his logic, so it didn't take long before the kitchen was back to its original pristine state.

"I've just got time to put the video on. There's a documentary I want to catch on the Third Reich," Cliff said, heading for the sitting room.

"We don't mind watching it, too." Mark told Cliff's retreating back.

"I need to tape it anyway. I might be able to use it sometime in class. I'm not sure if such a programme makes for a cosy night in with friends."

"I see your point," I said.

Cliff set up the recording. "I know most people are aware that the Nazis put Jews in concentration camps, but they also persecuted communists, the disabled, and homosexuals, too."

Mark nodded. "You're right, maybe tonight isn't the best time to watch such a programme."

Instead we sat around and listened to a few of Tom's jazz CDs. With the lights turned down low and the gas fire letting out plenty of heat, I felt snug and cosy.

"Do you think the music quality from a CD is better than vinyl or cassette?" I asked Tom when the first disc had finished playing.

"It's certainly better than tape, there's no hiss, but I'm still fond of my LPs."

"Luddite!" Cliff accused good-naturedly.

"I'm not. Vinyl gives warmth to a recording. Sometimes a CD can sound a bit too clinical."

"What do you think about getting a CD player as our present to each other this Christmas?" I asked Mark.

"That's a good idea," he said. "Do they lend out CDs at the library?"

"We started getting them in a year or two back."

Tom put in a second disc. I didn't get a look at the cover so wasn't sure what we were listening to, but it was pleasant enough.

Eventually our eyes began to grow heavy, so we decided to call it a night.

Chapter 3

"MISSED ME?" A grinning Sam asked as Mark and I were getting our bags out of the car.

"Not particularly." Mark shrugged.

Disappointment flashed over Sam's face, before it was replaced by a huge grin. "You're a rotten liar."

Mark couldn't maintain the pretence any longer and his grin began to match Sam's. "Can't kid you, can I?"

"Nah, I can read you too easily."

"Well, I don't know about you two, but I'd like to get inside and have a cup of coffee," I said, holding both bags, the boot lid still open.

"Sorry, Simon," Sam said, coming towards me and closing

the boot.

We walked into the house and I started the coffee maker.

"So, you two still managed to have a good time despite me not being there?" Sam asked.

"Well," Mark paused, "it wasn't easy, but I think we managed to."

"How are Tom and Cliff?" Sam asked.

"They're fine. They took Mark and me to a gay pub near them. We had a great time."

"Aw, I'd have liked to have gone with you."

"I don't think they'd have let you in. They don't have children's rooms in gay pubs," Mark said, ruffling Sam's hair.

"Geroff!" Sam dodged away. "I've just combed it."

"Aw, diddums," Mark teased.

Sam ran behind me. "Protect me!"

I turned round and put an arm over a giggling Sam's shoulders. "Did the nasty man frighten you?"

"Yes," Sam said, his face pressed to my shoulder.

I ruffled his hair, too.

"You're as bad as he is," a still giggling Sam said, stepping away.

"You can always go back home," Mark said.

Sam shrugged. "I think I can put up with you two for a bit longer."

"Gee, thanks," I said.

The coffee maker had done its thing, so I set about arranging the cups and got out a pack of chocolate chip cookies I'd been hiding.

"Double choc-chip, my favourite," Sam said.

"Mine, too. I thought we'd eaten them all?" Mark said, eyeing the packet hungrily.

"I love the 'we'…you're the cookie monster around here," I said. "I'm amazed you're not as big as a house, the number you munch your way through."

"I get plenty of exercise." He waggled his eyebrows.

"Mark! *Pas devant les enfants.*"

Sam sighed. "We had this conversation in Menorca. It's *'pas devant l'enfant,'* i.e., 'not in front of the child.' There's only one of me."

I shook my head. "Now the French lesson is over, I imagine we'll be stuck with you for Sunday dinner?"

"Earlier, Mum told me to get lost and 'get those two to feed you…for once,'" Sam said, giving a fair imitation of Helen.

"I'm sure she said nothing of the kind," Mark told him.

"Nah, I told her you promised to be back sometime this morning, and I asked her if I could eat with you. She said that, as I'd done all my homework yesterday, I could spend the day with you."

"That's more like the truth," I said.

"And speaking of Menorca," Mark said, "Tom sent over the photos he took while we were over there. Want to have a look?"

"Yeah. Any good ones?"

"One or two," I said, going through my bag to find the envelope.

"I might as well put a load of dirty laundry through the machine," Mark said, taking the bag once I'd extracted the packet of photographs.

"The clothes should get a chance to dry by this evening," I said, looking out of the kitchen window at the weather.

We heard a knock at the door. As Sam was busy looking through the photos and Mark was filling the washing machine, I went to see who was there.

"Billy." I smiled. "We haven't seen you in a couple of weeks."

"Hi, Simon. I had a bit of family stuff going on. My granny Patterson over in Manchester has been ill, and Mum and Dad have had to look around for a nursing home for her."

"Sorry to hear that."

"It's okay, she's been gaga for years now. I think the final straw was when she walked down her street in her night dress and flagged down a passing police car by waving one of her carpet slippers at it."

I tried to suppress a laugh. Billy saw my struggle, and began to laugh himself.

"It's all right, Mum and Dad have had a good chuckle over it, too. She'll be much better off now she can be looked after all the time."

We'd made our way into the kitchen by this point.

"Hi, Billy," Mark said.

"Hello, Mark." Turning to Sam, he asked, "What you got there?"

"Some photos of our holiday in Menorca."

I'd taken a few pictures with a disposable camera, but they hadn't come out all that well. Neither Mark nor I were particularly good photographers. Sam had taken a decent one of the church on Mount Toro, though.

"Ooh, let's have a varda."

"Varda?" Mark questioned.

"It means look in Polari," Billy said.

Mark and Sam looked confused.

"It was on the radio the other day. Simon, do you know about it?"

I nodded and explained about how, years ago, some gays and theatre people spoke a kind of dialect they called Polari.

"I've never heard of it," Mark said.

"It's almost defunct now."

Billy examined each of the pictures in the envelope which Sam had just given him.

"I like this one," he said, pointing at a photo of Sam sitting on Tom's shoulders in the swimming pool at the apartment complex. "Is that Tom you're sitting on?"

"Yeah, that's him. We had a load of fun together."

Billy also liked the one of Mark and me feeding each other breakfast. That was taken on our last day. Sam had stayed in Tom and Cliff's apartment that night. The next morning the three of them had come over, Tom carrying a basket with fresh fruit and a bag of rolls still warm from the oven.

They had made Mark and me go out onto the balcony and eat the honeymoon breakfast that Cliff was preparing in the kitchen. Tom then brought out a couple of glasses, which he'd filled with buck's fizz. Mark and I had had a fun time sipping each other's frothing orange juice and champagne with linked arms.

"Billy, do you want to eat Sunday dinner with us?" Mark's voice brought me back to the present.

"I told Mum that I was going to eat at Sam's."

"He's eating here. Do you two want to nip back to your house, Sam, and ask your mum if she'd pop round here if Billy's parents happen to ring?"

"Okay, that's a good idea," Billy said.

We knew Helen would run interference for Billy should his folks need to contact him. Billy hadn't come out to his parents, and Sam had accepted the fact that Billy was too nervous to out himself.

"And Sam? Ask your mum and dad if it's okay for us to take you to the beer garden at the Mucky Duck," Mark called out to the pair before they left the house.

THE FLORAL DISPLAYS in the beer garden were well past their best. Still, I thought they were doing pretty well, considering it was mid-October.

The boys had a biology test the next day at school. They were quizzing each other about the differences between arteries and veins. I'd taken human biology at A-level, and despite the fact I'd forgotten most of the information I'd so carefully stored away during my studies, I'd remembered enough to be of help to them.

"But I thought veins always carried de-oxygenated blood, you know from the body tissues?" Billy said with a puzzled expression.

"Yes," I said, "they do, but the four pulmonary veins carry oxygen-rich blood from the lungs back to the left auricle—sometimes called the left atrium—of the heart, through the mitral valve to the left ventricle, and then it's pumped into the aorta."

"Oh, right, have we done mit…" he asked Sam.

"Mitral valve," I corrected, hoping I wasn't sounding too much like a schoolteacher. "It's also called the bicuspid valve."

"Ah, right. I'm with you now," Billy said.

A little later, after we'd drained our glasses, Mark said, "Well, fellas, we better start making a move. That chicken will need to be put in the oven soon."

We made our way home. The topic of conversation had shifted to the state of the England football team.

"I bet you can't name any of the members of the England team, can you, Simon?" Sam asked.

I had to admit I couldn't. I wasn't interested in football at all. Although I did like looking at the players' thighs. But I thought I'd be better off keeping that piece of information to myself.

Once back at home, I hung out the washing, then got on with preparing the dinner while the others set up a board game.

"We're not playing that again, are we?" I said when I re-entered the living room.

They had gotten out the Monopoly board.

"I want to see if I can beat him," Mark said, pointing at a grinning Sam.

"Simon, are you going to be the old boot again?" Sam asked. "Cause it suits you."

"Come 'ere you cheeky little bugger!" I'd just sat on the sofa next to Mark. I got back up and whipped round the table to get at Sam. But before I got there, someone knocked on the door.

"Saved by the knock."

Sam squirmed in the chair he was crammed into with Billy. "Billy would have protected me."

"Would I?"

Sam dug Billy in the ribs.

"Oh, I would, I would." It was Billy's turn to squirm.

"Hi, Paul," I said when I'd opened the door. "Come in."

"Thanks, but I can't stop." He stood just inside the room. "Billy, your mum just rang. Your grandma is causing problems at the nursing home, so they—your mum and dad—have decided to go over there and see if they can sort it out."

"Did they say what happened?" Billy asked.

"Seems she's barricaded herself in her room and is claiming the staff are trying to poison her."

"Shit. Oh, sorry." Billy blushed.

"It's okay," Paul told him. "Your mum and dad think they'll have to stay in Manchester tonight. Your mum says you left your key on the rack."

Billy felt through his pockets. "Oh, shit! Sorry." His blush deepened.

Paul smiled and shook his head. "Your mum asked me to drive you home so you can get a few things together and sleep over at our place."

"I'm sixteen, they could have let me stop at home by myself."

Paul shrugged. "You'll have to take that up with them. Your dad said he wants to set off in a few minutes. So you need to get a move on."

Not unsurprisingly, Sam wanted to go with Billy to collect his stuff.

"Do you two still want to eat here?" Mark asked.

"Please," Sam said.

"It's quiet in here without the kids," I said once they'd all left.

Mark chuckled. "Why, have you got something in mind that'll make some noise?"

I did, and we both raced upstairs so I could show him.

ABOUT HALF AN hour later, two excited teenagers burst through the front door. Fortunately, Mark and I had just finished our fun and were coming down the stairs.

"Oi, you'll have the hinges off." Mark had to shout above the noise they were making.

"It's great! I'm so happy I could burst," Billy said.

"I hope you're not talking about your grandmother?" Mark asked.

"No, of course not!"

"Billy!" Both Mark and I said at the same time.

Billy's face fell. "I'm sorry. No, it isn't Gran. You tell 'em, Sam."

"Billy's parents know about us," Sam said. "I mean, they know we're boyfriends."

"And they're all right about it?" I asked.

Billy nodded.

"As you know, we went round to get his stuff," Sam said. "You know, so he could stay at my place. And his dad said Billy might as well stay with his boyfriend, rather than at his uncle's. You could have heard a pin drop then. I thought Billy was going to start crying, but his dad just hugged Billy and told him that his uncle Bill had let the cat out of the bag months ago. They were waiting for Billy to say something."

"Mum said she just wanted me to be happy." Billy sniffed and rubbed at his eyes.

"You don't look very happy," Mark said.

"I am, I'm just so relieved." He reached for Sam, who gave him a hug.

I was more than a little angry with Billy's Uncle Bill. He had promised to keep Billy's secret, but evidently he'd decided not to. The only saving grace as far as I was concerned was that it had all ended happily. But I thought it better to hold my tongue.

A saucepan started to boil over, so I went back into the kitchen to see to it and to get on with preparing the rest of the dinner. I could hear the others talking in the living room.

"You'll be able to stop more often at my house now," Billy said.

"Yes, but don't forget you're sitting your exams this year," Mark said. "I don't want to sound like a wet blanket, but if your grades start to drop, your parents will probably want to keep you apart till they improve again."

"You're probably right," Sam said, "though we are taking pretty much the same subjects."

"But how much of the time together will you spend studying, and how much snogging?"

Billy giggled.

"Just be sensible, that's all I'm saying," Mark said.

I continued to work, preparing vegetables, basting the chicken, and whipping up a chocolate sponge pudding.

Mark came into the kitchen and looked over my shoulder. "Can I lick the bowl out when you're done?"

I laughed. I used to ask my mum the same thing when she was baking. "Of course you can," I said, giving him a quick kiss. "I'll even leave a little in the bottom of the bowl."

He gave me a wide smile.

"It's quiet in there. What are the boys up to?" I asked.

"Probably getting in as much snogging as they can before they're made to study." He laughed.

"I heard you do your cautionary big-brother routine."

"You don't think I went too far, do you?"

I shook my head. "Not at all."

"Thanks. I just know that if they overdo it, their parents will get upset, and..."

"Exactly." I continued to mix the pudding batter. "I think we've got a carton of chocolate custard in the cupboard. Would you have a look?"

Mark rooted around, and came up with it. "I used to love chocolate pudding with chocolate sauce when we had it for school dinners."

"Me, too," I admitted. "It was about the only decent thing they made."

"Same at my school." Mark looked out of the kitchen window and said, "I think we'll be able to eat outside this afternoon. The sun is still shining and there's hardly any breeze."

"Why not? Like you said earlier, we won't get many more days with good weather this year."

Mark got out the cutlery, plates, glasses, and so on, and went out through the back door to set the table.

"YOUR DAD RECKONS we ought to dig up the last couple of yards of the lawn before winter sets in, if we want to use the ground to plant anything next spring," Mark said before putting a forkful of chicken into his mouth.

"Oh, right." I knew little about horticulture, leaving that side of things to Mark. "What were you thinking of growing?"

"Vegetables, mainly. It'd be nice to be able to pick our own, much fresher than buying them in the shops."

"Cheaper, too," Sam put in.

"Spoken like a true Yorkshireman," Mark grinned.

Though secretly I admitted to myself that Sam had a point.

"We'll need to buy a few garden tools," I said, mentally planning another trip to the garden centre.

"A spade, fork, and perhaps a hoe as well," Mark said.

"Can we go with you when you buy them?" Sam piped up.

I rolled my eyes. "You only want to go check out the checkout guy."

The others groaned at my weak pun.

"I don't think he works there anymore." Sam admitted.

"Oh?" Mark asked.

"Whenever I've been there with Mum and Dad, I couldn't find him."

"I imagine we'll be making a trip down there next weekend, so if your parents don't mind, you could both come with us," I said, picking up the dish of roast potatoes. "Anyone want another?"

Sam did, but Mark and Billy shook their heads.

Mark spent the rest of the meal outlining his plans for the garden next year. I must admit his efforts for this year had certainly brightened the place up. There wasn't much point in attempting anything fancy for the bit of ground at the front. It faced north, and the grass that was growing there was about all we could expect to thrive in such an inhospitable spot. Besides, it was such a small piece of ground.

After dinner, Sam and Billy offered to do the washing up, so Mark and I relaxed on the sofa in the front room.

"It's been a great weekend." I kicked off my shoes and rested my stocking feet in Mark's lap.

"It was good to see Tom and Cliff again." Mark started to massage my feet. "Don't think we'll get that close to Al and Keith though. They're just a bit too…I don't know, intense."

I nodded and closed my eyes. "Thanks for what you did in the pub when Keith made that comment about fresh meat. I was beginning to feel like I did in that nightclub we went to."

"I know, but Tom called them off; you felt okay after that, didn't you?"

I nodded again. "Thanks to you."

I twisted around so Mark and I were snuggled up together.

"You two at it again?" Sam said some time later, cutting in on our impromptu make-out session.

"Yes, so bugger off!" I told him. He just stood there and giggled.

"We've finished cleaning up," Billy said.

"Thanks. So what do you want to do now?" Mark asked.

"Can we play Monopoly?"

I groaned.

"I might let you win if you're especially nice to me," Sam promised.

"Since when have I ever been anything but especially nice to you?" I asked him.

"True," Sam said after a moment's hesitation.

"Cheeky sod." I would have gotten off the couch to cuff him around the ear, but I didn't have the energy.

"I suppose you want to play Monopoly as well?" Mark

asked Billy.

He smiled. "I want to see if I can get a row of hotels on Park Lane and Mayfair.

"Raving capitalist," Mark said. "Picking the two most expensive properties on the board."

The game was set up again, and we all gathered round. I made it plain from the start I wasn't going to be the old boot.

About forty-five minutes into the game, Paul knocked on our front door.

"Sam, your mum was wondering when you two were going to come back home?"

"Uh, Dad?"

I had my suspicions as to what was coming next.

Sam got up and hugged his father. "You are the best dad in the world, do you know that?"

A knowing smile came onto Paul's face. "You're the best son in the world."

"Do you think, as I've only got a single bed, and I'd hate for Billy and me to wake up Charlotte and everything and it would mean that you and mum wouldn't have to feed us supper, or breakfast tomorrow, if me and Billy stayed here tonight."

"Billy's parents were expecting him to sleep at our house."

"Yeah, but, Dad, he'd be much more comfortable in a double bed. You wouldn't want to make him have an uncomfortable night would you?"

Paul's smile got a little broader. "You're absolutely right, son. So you can sleep in your bed and Billy can sleep here."

I had to bite my lip to not burst out laughing at Sam's exasperated expression.

"Daaad!"

"Even if I was to agree to you two sleeping together, purely for reasons of comfort of course," Paul added, "there's one small but important thing you've forgotten."

"Huh?"

"You haven't asked Simon and Mark if you and Billy can

sleep here tonight."

Sam dipped his head and came to sit next to me. "Simon?"

"What can I do for you, Sam?"

"Can me and Billy stay in your spare room tonight?"

I chose not to correct Sam's bad grammar, but couldn't let the lack of manners pass. Call me old-fashioned. "And what's the magic word?"

"Pleeeease," he said with all earnestness.

"Okay, okay. You can stay; those puppy dog eyes of yours do it every time," I admitted.

"Yes! I knew I'd have no problem convincing you."

"Bet you didn't," Mark chuckled.

LATER THAT EVENING, after we'd sent the boys to bed, I turned to Mark. "Now where were we earlier this afternoon before we were interrupted?"

"I don't know, perhaps I need reminding." He smiled.

We spent the next goodness knows how long just kissing and caressing each other, and watching the embers of the fire slowly fade.

Chapter 4

I WAS IMMERSED in an "absolutely riveting" study on the nationally declining standards of literacy in Britain when Mary stuck her head round the door of my office.

"Got a minute?"

"Of course." I smiled at her and dropped the report on my desk. "I could do with the distraction. This guy," I tapped the report, "has developed the fine art of using a paragraph when a single sentence would do."

Mary smiled. "It's just, we haven't seen as much of each other as we used to."

"I know, the promotion, both of us finding our ideal men, etc., etc."

Mary and I worked at the local library. Until I got a promotion we'd worked in the same department. But since I'd been made up to senior librarian we saw a lot less of each other.

Mary seated herself in my guest chair and crossed her legs. "I was wondering if you and Mark wanted to go out somewhere. Maybe this weekend?"

I remembered the last time Mark and I had spent the evening with Mary and her boyfriend, Jerry. It hadn't been all that comfortable. Jerry was gorgeous to look at, and he seemed to have conquered his homophobia, but Mark and I had agreed not to repeat the experience. We didn't feel comfortable around the man.

Mary continued. "Jerry's staying in York this weekend, flat-hunting. He thought he'd got somewhere sorted for his final year, but it fell through at the last minute."

Jerry was a graduate student at York University.

"So Mark and I were a backup plan, then?" I grinned, partially out of relief.

"How did you guess?" she laughed.

"Okay then, we'll get our heads together later and see what we can come up with."

She stood. "I'll let you get back to your report."

"Gee, thanks."

FOR THE PAST couple of months Mark had been taking driving lessons. At first I'd tried to teach him, but it hadn't worked.

I'd driven to a large disused industrial estate to give Mark some practice in manoeuvring the car round corners, reversing, and parking.

At one point I'd seen we were heading towards a telephone pole. "I think you should swerve round this," I'd said, trying to keep the unease out of my voice all the while pressing my foot against a brake pedal I'd wished was present.

Mark had turned the steering wheel abruptly, which had

jolted me in my seat. A box of tissues, a pen and a few coins had fallen onto the floor near my feet.

"Whoops, I think I was a bit heavy handed."

"Just a tad," I'd said, trying to stay calm.

Although nothing had gone disastrously wrong during the practice, the last thing Mark needed was for me to become tense or lose my temper, so we'd decided he should find a driving instructor.

Once we'd got home I called Ted, the guy who had done the mini-refresher course with me, and he'd agreed to take Mark on as a client.

Mark had sat his first test about a month earlier. Unfortunately he'd gotten in a terrible mess while trying to reverse into a parking space.

We thought Mark would benefit from a few more lessons before taking his test again. It wasn't until the day after I'd spoken to Mary that the date for his second test arrived.

Mark had arranged a late afternoon slot so he wouldn't have to take time off. He worked at the café a couple of doors down from the library. I was sure Daphne—the café owner—would have let Mark go early as she thought the world of him. I think he brought out the mothering instinct in her.

I kept looking up at the wall clock in my office. I'm sure I was far more nervous than Mark. The time seemed to move with leaden slowness. I tried to occupy my mind with work, but it was no good. I was trying to write down my opinions on the report I'd read the day before, but I just couldn't get the words to flow. So many pieces of paper had been scrunched up and discarded that my wastepaper basket was full.

The clock eventually dragged its way round to a quarter to five. I'd expected to hear from Mark by four at the latest. In typical Simon Peters fashion I began to panic, thinking he'd been involved in an accident, had failed the test and was too upset to tell me, or some other terrible calamity had befallen him. My rising sense of dread evaporated when Mark stuck his head around my door.

"Where have you been? I was worried sick," I said, getting to my feet.

"Aren't you going to ask me how I did?"

"Sorry," I gave him a hug.

"They were running really late at the test centre."

"Well?"

He pulled a piece of paper out of his back pocket and waved it at me. "I passed!"

"I'm so proud of you." I gave him a deep kiss on the lips.

"Ooops," Mary said, backing out of my office.

"Come in, silly," I said. "Mark's just passed his driving test, and I was congratulating him."

"Great! Can I congratulate you, too?"

They kissed.

"You two better not be using tongues!" I mock-threatened.

They both laughed.

"I came to find out where you two wanted to go this weekend," Mary asked. "We'll have to turn it into a celebration, now."

"How about we go somewhere nice for a meal?" I suggested. "You can drive there, Mark, but I'll drive back so you can have a drink."

"But every time we've been out in the past, you've had to stick to soft drinks. Now you should reap the benefit."

"We can do that next time. Tomorrow is your celebration." I kissed him again.

"Okay then, where?" Mary asked.

"There's that new Italian place just opened up on the road to York," Mark suggested.

"Like I said, it's your celebration, so if that's where you want to go, that's where we'll go."

I looked up the number, called the restaurant, and booked a table.

❖

"NOW YOU'VE PASSED your test, I want you to take the car to work each morning," I told Mark as we were cleaning up after dinner that evening. We often seemed to hold conversations at the kitchen sink.

"Why?"

"Because you have to go in early, and with the shorter days now I don't like the idea of you walking the streets in the dark. You can leave the car parked and I'll bring it home at night. It'll always be light for you walking home at three. Though if it's raining hard, take the car home, and if you can, come back and pick me up."

"I'm a big boy now. I can walk to work."

"I know you are." I squeezed the ample bulge in his trousers. "But just humour me, okay?"

"I need some persuading." Mark pushed his crotch into my hand. The dirty dishes were forgotten while I worked on getting my man to see things my way.

"Hello!" It was Sam. He had his own key and, from the sound of it, had let himself in.

Mark and I parted just as Sam entered the kitchen.

"Billy's mum and dad are away in Manchester again this weekend, and...Mark, why're the front of your trousers wet?"

"We were, uh, just washing up and..." Changing the subject I asked, "What did you say about Billy's parents being away?"

"Huh?" Sam managed to shift his gaze from Mark's crotch. "They wanted him to go with them, but he managed to wriggle out of it."

"And?" I knew where Sam was going, but decided to play dumb.

"And we were both wondering if we could stop here this weekend?"

"Only if Billy gets permission from his parents to sleep here," Mark told him. "I know we bent the rules Sunday night, but I'm not happy about doing that again."

I nodded my agreement.

"Yeah." Sam sighed. "We thought you'd say that. Billy said he'd ask his mum to ring you. I just hope she does."

"Okay, we'll wait for her call." Then I remembered the meal we'd booked at the Italian restaurant. "Mark and I won't be in on Friday evening, so you two will have to stay at your house that night."

"Where are you going?" Sam asked.

"Nosy little bugger," Mark said, tapping Sam's nose.

"Yeah, so where are you off to?"

We laughed.

"I forgot to tell you," Mark said. "I've passed my driving test. So Simon and I are going out for a slap-up meal with Mary to celebrate."

"Wow, that's great! Congratulations." Sam got that look on his face, and I knew he was up to something. "But you can't have a proper celebration without me and Billy."

I chuckled. "Nice try, but no chance."

Sam looked to Mark, no doubt hoping for a different answer.

Mark shook his head. "Not this time." Then he smiled. "But tell you what. Saturday the four of us will do something fun together." Mark looked over at me for agreement.

I nodded. "You and Billy can help us choose if you like."

Sam smiled. "Thanks."

"Now bugger off home." I grinned. "You've got school in the morning, and…"

"And you want to get back into Mark's trousers." Sam finished, which wasn't far off the truth.

"Say goodnight, Sam," Mark said.

"Goodnight, Sam," Sam said. He gave us both a quick hug and then left.

Now, where were we?" I waggled my eyebrows at Mark.

He picked up my hand and pressed it against his crotch.

"Ah, yes, I remember now," I said, falling to my knees and lowering his zip to get a better look at what I'd be working with.

I LOVED THAT we closed the library half an hour early on Fridays. And for once, the day seemed to fly by.

"Mary, we'll pick you up about quarter past seven, okay?" I said as I stood in the queue behind her to sign out.

"I'll be ready."

I doubted that, but kept my opinion to myself. I'd allowed a little extra time in the schedule to accommodate Ms Bartlett's legendary lack of timekeeping.

AMAZINGLY, MARY WAS ready when Mark pulled up outside her parents' house.

"Good grief, woman," I said to her when she got into the backseat. "I thought we'd have to drag you out with your heated rollers still in."

"Daft bugger, I don't need rollers." She fingered her hair. "It's naturally curly."

"And a new dress, too," Mark said.

"I've got to make the effort now and again."

"And we're deeply honoured," I said over my shoulder.

Mary stuck her tongue out at me.

❖

WE WERE LED to our table by the maître d', a handsome older Italian gentleman. I wondered if the French term was appropriate in an Italian restaurant. Whatever his title, he pulled out Mary's chair and waited for her to sit.

"Thank you," Mary said, trying to stifle a giggle.

"Your waiter, Giuseppe, will be with you shortly." He handed out menus. "Would you care for anything from the bar?"

After taking our drinks order, the man bowed and departed.

"He's nice," Mary whispered.

"And too old for you," I observed, opening my menu.

"True." Mary sighed and opened her menu.

"It's all in Italian." Mark whispered to me.

"What did you expect?" I said, smiling above my menu at Mark. "We're in an Italian restaurant." I took pity on him then. "The English translation is towards the back."

Mary giggled again. I was beginning to wonder if she'd been at the sherry before coming out.

A man, Giuseppe I assumed, approached our table. "Are you ready to order?" He smiled at us, but saved the biggest one for Mary.

"Uh, yes," she giggled.

Apparently this was a family-owned restaurant, because Giuseppe was a younger version of the maître d'.

We made our choices, although Mary seemed to need a little help deciding, something Giuseppe was most happy to provide.

"And the wine?" Giuseppe asked once he'd noted our food order.

I'd always found choosing the right wine to go with a meal quite daunting. I turned to the wine list and began to scan its contents, paying more attention to the prices than the varieties.

"What would you recommend, Giuseppe?" Mary asked. "It's okay to call you that, isn't it?"

He seemed charmed. "Of course." He suggested some wine which meant nothing to me.

I nodded my agreement but explained I'd have a sparkling mineral water instead.

Giuseppe, just like his older relative, bowed slightly and departed.

"He isn't too old for me," Mary said, watching the waiter depart.

Mark sniggered. "What would Jerry say?"

Mary sighed. "True. Maybe Jerry would demand satisfaction from Giuseppe and they'd fight a duel over me." She giggled.

"You seem full of life this evening," Mark observed.

"I'm happy that the work week is over and I can sleep in for the next couple of mornings."

The conversation continued to flow as we waited for our food. The place was pretty full, but because the tables weren't placed too close together, I didn't feel hemmed in.

Mary and I started to reminisce about the old days in non-fiction. Mary told Mark some of the more comic aspects of what we used to get up to.

"Oh, Simon, I forgot to tell you." Mary giggled. "Last week a man came in to the department and asked if we had any books on suicide. I was tempted to tell him he couldn't borrow them because he wouldn't bring them back."

It took a couple of seconds for the penny to drop. Then I laughed, clapping a hand over my mouth to muffle the noise.

"I don't get it," Mark said.

I explained. But since it had to be spelled out, Mary's joke lost much of its humour.

"I hope he didn't really want to kill himself," Mark said.

"I'm pretty sure it was for an essay he was writing," Mary reassured him.

Mark nodded and took a sip from his glass.

"One thing, though," Mary said, picking up her own glass. "I haven't seen Fred in a few days. I hope he's all right."

I told Mark that Fred was the town tramp, and how he would occupy his seat nearest the radiator in the reading room for most of the day.

Our food arrived, and conversation faltered as we ate. I had to admit, the food was excellent. Although I hadn't been all that adventurous and just ordered a plate of spaghetti with a meat sauce. The garlic bread, which we all shared, was the best I'd ever tasted.

Throughout the meal, Giuseppe kept returning to the table to replenish our basket of bread, refill the bowl of olives, that kind of thing. Each time he'd smile at Mary; later in the meal he even began to flirt a little with her. Mary would giggle, smile, and flirt back.

After yet another visit, this time to refresh my water glass, I said, "I think Jerry should order a pair of duelling pistols."

Mary laughed. "Oh, to be fought over by two handsome men. It'd be just like in a historical romance novel."

"Would the beautiful lady care for dessert?" Giuseppe asked Mary when he came to clear away the dinner plates. I noticed he hadn't asked either Mark or me.

"I've got to watch my figure," she said, giggling yet again.

"In Italy we like ladies who are…" He made enlarging gestures with his hands.

Mary smiled. "Perhaps you have some ice cream?"

"We have some delicious spumoni…only the best for the beautiful lady." He then must have remembered his manners and turned to us. "Sirs?"

Mark and I decided to go with the ice cream, too, especially when Giuseppe told us his mother had made it herself the day before.

Giuseppe soon returned to the table with three bowls, though I would have sworn the one he placed in front of Mary had more in it.

After the waiter had left, I said, "He's trying to fatten you up so you meet his idea of what a woman should look like."

She reddened slightly.

After we finished dessert and had declined the offer of coffee, I asked for the bill.

Giuseppe returned with a leather folder for me and a single red rose for Mary.

"A beautiful rose, for a beautiful young lady." He bowed over Mary's hand and gave it a chaste kiss.

After I signed the credit card slip, and—thanks to Mary's quiet but insistent prompting—added a generous tip, the three of us got to our feet. Mary thanked Giuseppe for a wonderful dinner. He asked her—and us, too I suppose—to come again soon.

"I will," Mary promised. Then she had to break the poor

man's heart by adding, "I'll ask my boyfriend to bring me."

"DID YOU HAVE a nice time, even though you left me behind?" Sam asked with a grin.

"Yes thanks, we had a great time," I said, choosing not to react to the second part of his remark.

"What's on the agenda for today?" Sam asked.

"Cleaning the house, then the garden centre," Mark said.

"Oh, right," Billy said. "If we give you a hand with the cleaning, you'll finish sooner."

"True. That's very kind of you," I said.

"S'okay." Sam shrugged.

So the house got cleaned in record time. I chose to tackle the kitchen. Mark did the living room, and the boys tidied things upstairs. We each had to wait until the vacuum cleaner was free, but other than that, everything ran like clockwork.

IT BEING CLOSE to the end of the growing season, there weren't many people looking around the garden centre. Some of the items we needed were being sold off, so I didn't have to spend as much as I'd thought.

"Why're you smiling?" Mark asked.

I shrugged. "Oh, just happy to be out with my husband." This was true, but the savings I'd made had certainly added to my mood, too.

Mark shook his head. "If we leave the trolley here we'll be able to see it while we eat."

Sam had persuaded us to have lunch in the garden centre's café. As breakfast seemed hours ago, Mark and I agreed.

The cheeseburgers looked good, so all four of us chose them.

"You're right, Sam," Mark said after swallowing his first bite.

"That cute checkout guy doesn't seem to work here anymore."

Billy giggled.

We took our purchases home, and Mark stored them under a tarpaulin in the back yard.

"You'll be wanting a shed next, I suppose," I told him.

"Well," he smiled, "it'd come in handy."

I was later to learn just how handy.

The boys decided they wanted to go ice skating for their celebration of Mark passing his test. This wouldn't have been my first choice, but I was happy to go along with the majority decision. As the closest rink was some distance away, the boys agreed we'd wait until the next day to go.

Chapter 5

SATURDAY AFTERNOON, AND with little else to do, everyone settled down and watched sport on the television. I wasn't much of a sport-orientated person, so I curled up in a corner and carried on with the book I had started a few days earlier. I managed to filter out the noise from the TV and the comments the others were making.

"Do you want dinner now?" Mark's voice broke in on my literary daydream.

I looked over at the clock. It was a little past five.

"Okay, I'll go see what we've got."

"The boys said they'd make something."

"Oh, right," I said.

I could hear the clatter of pots and pans coming from the

other room, along with the odd giggle from the chefs.

"Boys!" Mark called out. "Get your hands off each other and back onto the food."

They laughed.

A short while later, Billy popped his head round the door to tell us the food was ready.

All four of us sat down to a meal of cottage pie, carrots, and peas. We'd had some minced beef in the freezer, and the boys must have used that as a base for the pie.

"This is great. Thank you," I said.

Sam and Billy beamed at the praise.

Mark nodded. "Mind you, we already know Sam can cook because he made us breakfast a few times when he stayed with us."

This brought up the subject of when Sam's parents went away and he stayed with us.

"That's when you two found out about each other, wasn't it?" I asked.

Sam nodded. "I can still remember your face when you outed yourself and Mark to Billy. You could have fried eggs on your cheeks, they were glowing so much."

I'd come home from the library for dinner and called out something sexy—more like stupid—to Mark, not knowing Billy was in the kitchen. I could see the humour in the situation now, but at the time I'd been pretty mortified.

"Because of that, I was able to find my Sam," Billy said, wrapping an arm around his boyfriend.

"And I found you." Sam kissed Billy.

"Not at the table, you'll give me indigestion," Mark said.

"Shut up. I think it's lovely," I said.

"THE NIGHTS ARE getting colder," I observed as we walked to the pub after dinner. "I think we should put the thicker duvet on the bed tonight." I pulled up the collar of my coat.

Mark put an arm around my waist. There weren't many streetlights, and few people were out and about.

After waiting for about ten minutes we managed to get a table in the children's room.

The family who'd occupied the table previously had left when the older brother pushed his younger sister, making her cry.

"That's it!" the father had slapped the side of the kid's head, pushing him into his sister. "James, I've bloody well warned you for the last time, now we're going home, and you can fucking forget about watching the bloody telly tomorrow, too."

James had put up a protest, which was still in full flow as the father dragged him through the outside door.

Sam and Billy quickly ran to claim the table; Mark and I followed with the drinks that Mark had just brought through from the main bar.

"Seems like a nice family," I said.

"James is a third year at our school," Sam said. "He's always being told off for fighting. I bet Mrs Jones, the headmistress, will expel him next time."

"He's had a couple of suspensions already," Billy added.

"Nice," Mark said.

Sam opened his packet of crisps. "He's got an older brother who left school a couple of years ago. I think he's in prison now for burgling houses."

I shook my head. "Sounds like a wonderful family all-round."

When we'd arrived, the boys had put their names on the blackboard to play pool. So they left our table when their turn came up.

"Want another?" Mark asked, draining his glass.

"Please."

I got up, asked the boys if they wanted the same again, and went into the main bar. There was a bit of a queue. The barmaid was new, and wasn't all that efficient, which didn't help. She was obviously employed for assets other than her barkeeping abilities. So great were these assets they were barely held in check by the tight blouse she was wearing. Some of the other male patrons were taking full advantage of the view, asking her to reach down to the bottom shelf for various things.

"What will it be, Simon?" Ron had appeared.

"Hi, Ron." I gave my order, and he began to pump the beer and dispense the soft drinks for the boys.

"New barmaid?" I asked.

"Yeah. She seems to be a hit," Ron said with barely concealed irritation.

I smiled. "Well, if it increases trade."

Ron rolled his eyes. "It was the brewery's idea to get in some extra help. Though between you and me, she's not that much help."

"Oh dear," I said, handing Ron the money for the drinks.

He gave me my change, and I went back into the children's room carrying the tray. I gave the boys their drinks, then went on to the table and took my seat next to Mark.

"Did you see the barmaid?" he asked.

"Could hardly fail to."

He laughed.

We spent a couple of hours in the pub, Sam and Billy coming back to join us after their game was finished. At one point Sam had to fend off the advances of Trudy, a teenage girl who by the looks of things wanted to get to know Sam quite intimately. Goodness knew where her parents were. And I'd have thought Billy would have become upset, but I was proved totally wrong. He found Trudy's wandering hands and probing questions really amusing.

I eventually took pity on Sam and announced that we ought to head off home. Sam looked gratefully at me as he disengaged himself from Trudy's clutches.

"She was like an octopus," Sam admitted when we were walking home. "She had her hands everywhere." He shivered, and I didn't think it was from cold.

Billy laughed. "Couldn't you take it?"

"I'll pass her on to you if you like. I'll tell her at school on Monday that you've got the hots for her."

"Don't you dare!" Billy said, chasing after a giggling Sam.

"We'd better get some more milk," I told Mark as we neared the corner shop.

I went to the refrigerated food section and picked up a four-pint carton of whole milk. They also stocked semi and fully skimmed, but frankly, if God had intended us to drink that muck, he wouldn't have given us taste buds.

"Can we get a thick-sliced loaf, too, please?" Sam asked. "I want some toast tonight."

BACK AT HOME, Sam got out the toasting fork and settled himself in front of the glowing coals. Once his toast was ready, he spread it with the butter that Mark had brought from the kitchen. Sam then handed the slice to Billy.

I gave Sam a quick smile of approval.

After finishing off most of the loaf, the boys went upstairs to prepare for bed.

"Those two are the cutest," I said to Mark.

He smiled and then leaned in to kiss me. "Finally we get some time to ourselves."

"SIMON, LET GO of the rail!" Sam sniggered.

"At least while I'm holding it, I'm upright. And whose daft idea was it to come to an ice rink in the first place?" I asked, letting go for a moment just to see if I could remain on my feet.

"That's it!" Billy said, coming to support me on my other side. "You're getting the hang of it now."

By the end of an hour I was able to move in one direction and stay on my feet. However, I hadn't mastered turns, and braking was problematic, too. The others seemed to be having a whale of a time. Sam and Billy were weaving all over the place. The rink was crowded, it being the weekend, so none of us were able to get up much of a head of steam. Not that I had any intention of going fast.

Each time Mark's eyes met mine across the ice, my insides warmed. Still after all this time, I found myself marvelling that the man who was looking so adoringly over at me wanted to share his life with me.

By the time our ice time had run out, I'd managed to perform some pretty basic manoeuvres. However, I knew my earlier clumsiness would leave me with some bruising. That ice was bloody hard!

We handed back our skates to the female attendant who was too busy filing her nails to take much notice of us.

Once we'd passed her booth, Mark said, "Did you see that ring on her finger?"

"Yeah, why?" I asked.

"I didn't think it was possible to be both vacant and engaged at the same time."

All four of us roared with laughter—we even drew a few odd looks—which didn't quell our mirth.

"Now boys," Mark said from the driver's seat, "I know we're invited out to dinner at your place, Sam, but that won't be for another few hours. How's about refuelling at a burger joint?"

The boys agreed, so Mark pointed the car to the nearest Golden Arches.

Mark's driving was getting better and better. I knew it wouldn't be long before he'd do most of the driving when we were both together. He just seemed to have a natural feel for the road, something I knew I lacked.

"It was in McDonald's that Mary met Jerry," I told the boys as we sat in our booth, bags of burgers and fries on the table in front of us.

I told them about how awestruck Mary was, recalling that

I'd never seen quite such a glazed expression before.

The boys giggled.

"Okay." Mark closed his empty polystyrene burger container. "We'll get back, and you two can finish any last-minute homework before we eat at Paul and Helen's."

The boys groaned.

"Come on, it isn't that bad, surely?" I asked.

"Geography's so boring," Billy said.

"A lot depends on the teacher, I guess," Mark said, getting up from the table and picking up our rubbish and empty drink cups.

I knew their geography teacher. Mr Williams was one of those people who were biding their time till their pensions were due. It had been the best part of twenty years since he had taught me, and he was even planning what he'd do with his free time back then. He was heavily into fly-fishing. If the lesson got too boring, as it invariably did with both the subject and Mr Williams' dull delivery, all we had to do was ask him if he'd caught anything good recently.

His old—because to our teenage eyes he was ancient—face would light up and he'd regale us with yet another tale of the one that got away.

MUCH OF THE journey home was spent with the boys quizzing each other on their geography homework. The subject didn't really interest me. I'd dropped it after O-level, I didn't want to take the subject at A-level, and there was no way I was going to spend another two years in Fishy Willy's company.

Back at home, Sam went to his house for his books, and the two of them spent most of the time until dinner going over the main highlights of the inland waterways surrounding Britain's second city, Birmingham.

Looking over at the mantle clock, I said, "I'm nipping upstairs for a quick wash, then once Mark's done the same, we'll leave for your house, Sam."

"Who said I need a wash?" Mark joked.

"Get up those stairs, you dirty bugger."

"See what I've got to put up with?" Mark said to the boys. "Hen-pecked, that's what I am."

I threw a cushion at him.

"JUST IN TIME. Dinner will be on the table in a couple of minutes," Helen said once she'd let us in. "Go into the front room. Paul's in there minding Charlotte."

"Hi, guys," Paul greeted us. "Had a good time?" he asked Sam.

"We went to the ice rink. It was great." Sam smiled. "But I bet Simon will be sore tomorrow."

"Fell over a few times?" Paul laughed.

"Just a few," I said.

Mark leaned in and whispered, "I promise I'll give you a good rub down when we get home."

I felt my face heat and pushed him away.

My attention was taken by Charlotte, who crawled over to me and tugged on my trouser leg. "Aw, aren't you beautiful?"

Sam picked her up and put her on my knee. She smiled up at me.

"You've got a fan there," Paul said with pride.

"You like your uncle Simon?" I asked, bouncing the little girl on my knee.

Charlotte responded with a giggle.

"She's more fun now than she used to be," Sam admitted.

I smiled over at him, knowing how he'd struggled to accept his younger sister.

"At first she didn't do much apart from cry, sleep, crap, and drink milk."

I laughed. "You're not crying now are you?" I bounced her again and was rewarded with another smile and a gurgle.

I felt dampness on my knee. Putting my hand near the most likely cause confirmed it.

"Um, Charlotte's, uh, I think she needs to be changed." I looked around for someone to take her.

"I'll do it," Sam said, scooping her up and taking her out of the room.

Paul smiled. "He's really come around to her now. Thanks to you two."

Mark shook his head. "I think he just liked that he could come over to our house if things got too much for him."

"I'm sure you've done a lot more than just provide an escape route," Paul said.

"We told Sam that he ought to be nice to her, as she'll be the only source of grandchildren for you," I said.

Paul laughed. "There is that, I suppose."

"Dinner's ready," Helen called out.

We all made our way towards the wonderful smells coming from the kitchen.

Sam and Billy were already sitting at the table when we entered.

"Charlotte was tired, so I put her in her cot for a bit," Sam told Paul.

We began to tuck into Helen's great cooking. As was common in Yorkshire, the Yorkshire pudding was the first course. The traditional roast beef of old England, with all the trimmings, followed.

After we'd cleaned our plates, Helen said, "there's some chocolate cake in the tin if anyone wants any."

No one could face the prospect of further food, so we all politely declined.

"Hey, love," Paul said, rubbing at his belly, which still looked pretty flat to me. "Simon and Mark took the boys to the skating rink today." Turning to Mark and me he added, "Helen and I first met at the rink."

"Don't remind me," Helen said. "It's the first and only time I fell at a boy's feet."

We laughed.

"Me and a bunch of mates from the cricket team had decided to go skating," Paul told us.

"And I'd gone with my next door neighbour. I'd never been on skates before, and I wasn't making too good a job of it. I'd decided to let go of the side rail and see what happened. Well, Paul happened." She smiled.

"Nice," Billy said.

"I wasn't much good on skates either," Paul admitted. "I just turned round, and a beautiful young lady just fell at my feet. Of course I did the gentlemanly thing and helped her up. We got talking, left the ice, and went for a coffee. I asked her for her phone number and I gave her mine. And the rest, as they say, is history."

"Aw, that's a nice story," I said.

Helen smiled wistfully. Then she turned to us. "You never told us exactly how you two got together."

Mark's face fell. "We bumped into each other in the street."

"But you came home from the hospital to live at Simon's. It must have been some bump," she persisted.

Mark continued to look uncomfortable.

Thankfully Paul intervened. "I think I can squeeze in a slice of that cake after all."

"Me, too," Billy added.

Helen got up from the table.

"Let me help you stack the dishwasher," I said.

"It's okay, it'll only take me a minute." Helen brought the cake and a couple of plates back to the table.

"If you're sure, we'll say goodbye, then. Simon's expecting a call from his Gran soon." Mark stood.

I gave his hand a quick squeeze of reassurance. I'd told Gran we were eating out and that I'd call her when we got home.

After thanking Helen for an excellent meal, and promising the boys we'd see them in the week, we left the Bates's and walked the couple of doors back to our place.

Safe in the front room, I put my arms around Mark and gave him a hug.

"Thanks," he said, returning the hug. "I don't think I'm ready to tell them yet. I'm glad Tom and Cliff know, but somehow I knew they'd understand."

I kissed his cheek.

"I love you."

"Love you more," I replied.

"Silly bugger." This brought a smile to Mark's lips, which I'd intended. My man's face grew even more beautiful when he smiled.

Chapter 6

IT TOOK ME a couple of hours to wade through the Monday morning paperwork, which as usual had magically appeared on my desk over the weekend.

After scaling the paper mountain, I paid a quick visit to my old stomping ground of non-fiction.

"Come to check up on me?" John smiled from his seat behind the counter.

John had gotten my old job when I'd been promoted.

I smiled and shook my head. "If you were doing anything wrong, Mary would have you bent over this desk, giving you a couple of whacks with a back number of the *Reader's Digest.*"

He laughed. "Yeah, you're right, she would."

"She would what?" Mary asked, coming around the corner.

"I was just telling John about your sadomasochistic streak."

"Don't you be giving away all my secrets. A girl has to maintain a certain air of mystery."

John laughed.

"The reason for my coming down to rub shoulders with the workers—"

"Huh!" Mary harrumphed.

"—was to find out if Fred had turned up today."

Mary's face instantly fell. She shook her head. "I don't think we've seen anything of him for about a week." She looked over at John, who nodded in agreement.

I sighed, knowing something had to be seriously wrong. "I'll ring round and see what I can find out."

"Thanks," Mary said.

I went back to my office and got out my dog-eared copy of the authority's directory of telephone extensions. I made a mental note to order a more up-to-date copy. I was certain that many of the numbers had changed since the book was printed.

After looking up the number for Social Services I gritted my teeth as I was placed into a game of telephone ping-pong, with me as the ball. First I was passed to an extension that was silent, then, when I called the number again, the receptionist put me through to a different extension. This one at least rang…and rang. Hanging up, I tried a third time. It reminded me of the time I'd called to report a broken streetlight just outside the library. I'd ended up being put through to someone in cleansing, otherwise known as the dustbin department.

The ringing stopped and was followed by a brusque, "Miss Marchant."

"Hello. I hope I'm still with Littleborough Social Services and not the street lighting department or something."

"This is Social Services."

"Thank goodness," I sighed, then went on to tell her who I was and what I was calling about.

"I'm sorry," she interrupted me, "we can't give out information like that to anyone who isn't a relative."

"But as far as we know he doesn't have any, the man's a tramp, a vagabond, vagrant, someone of no fixed abode." I closed my eyes and pinched the bridge of my nose, hoping I wasn't starting with a headache.

This got me absolutely nowhere with the social worker, or whoever she was, who kept insisting she couldn't pass on any information. I visualised a rather severe iron-grey haired schoolmistress-type, complete with steel-rimmed spectacles, something out of a girl's public school movie.

"Well, thank you so much. You've been so helpful," I said with as much sarcasm as I could muster.

"There's no need to take that tone. Client confide—"

I slammed the phone down on the officious Miss Bossyknickers Marchant and let out a long breath. My eyes fell again on the open phone directory.

"Of course!" I said, as a flash of inspiration hit.

I picked up the phone again and dialled Gillian Streeter, the personal assistant to the Director of Social Services. Gillian and my mother had met at secretarial college, and had remained firm friends ever since. Gillian used to babysit me when Mum and Dad had a night out.

The telephone connection was made; it rang a couple of times before a cultured female voice answered. "Good morning, Director's Office, Social Services."

"Auntie Gill, it's Simon Peters."

There was a brief pause, then, "Simon? I haven't heard your voice in such a long time. How are you doing?"

"I'm very well, thank you, Auntie Gill. How are you?"

Gillian wasn't my real auntie; she was much better. When she came over to babysit me, she'd wait until Mum and Dad had gone out, then she'd have a feel around in her capacious handbag. I knew what was coming next, and I always grew more excited the longer it took her to produce the small bag of sweets she always had in there. I'm sure she deliberately took longer than was necessary to locate the pear drops, liquorice allsorts, wine gums, or whatever it happened to be that day, thus prolonging my pleasure of expectation. I must have only been about three or four years old when this little scene first began to play itself out.

Gill and I chatted for a while, catching up on old news. She hadn't heard from mum in a month or so, so I filled in what little items of news I had remembered from the conversations I'd had with my mother.

Changing the subject, she said, "It's about time you got yourself settled with a nice girl."

I didn't want to tell her about Mark and me; I knew somehow she'd be disappointed, but in any case it wasn't the time to come out. It wasn't very brave of me, and I hated denying my love for Mark. I made some bland—and not terribly convincing—response about being busy at work, what with my promotion and everything.

It was time to introduce the reason why I was ringing her, so I told her about the non-appearance of Fred and that we were worried about him.

"I tried to get some information out of Miss Marchant at the local office, but I think it'd have been easier to get blood out of a stone."

"Ah," she laughed. "But first impressions aren't always the most reliable. If Miss Marchant had an endangered child on her caseload, she'd fight tooth and nail to make sure they were safe."

"Okay." I thought about calling Miss Marchant back to apologise. "Can you see if you can find anything out—about Fred, I mean? He's kind of like one of the family. And if he's in hospital, then I'm sure some of us would want to visit him."

"Of course I will. Give me an hour or so."

After hanging up, I scaled another paper mountain that had somehow magically appeared. Did papers have the ability to breed?

I'd no sooner started my climb when I was asked to make an appearance in the fiction section.

"Thank you for coming down, Mr Peters," Sally Timpson said to me when I appeared at her counter. "This reader has brought back a damaged library book but says it was like that when she borrowed it."

One of my less pleasant duties was to intervene if a book was brought back damaged and the reader refused to take responsibility. Turning to the reader I recognised her from the children's room at the pub; she was James's mother.

"I told you it was like that when I took it out," the woman said, ignoring me.

I asked to see the book—a large print copy of Jack Higgins's *The Eagle Has Landed*. The spine was hanging off, and it smelled pretty unpleasant, too. Opening the book, I discovered several damp and dark stains toward the rear.

I turned to the woman. "Mrs?"

"Thompson."

"When you borrowed this book, I assume you took it from the shelf?" I pointed to the library's admittedly meagre collection of large-print titles. "Then you brought it to this desk to have it stamped?" I flipped to the first page. Surprise, surprise, it was overdue.

"Course."

"Every time a book is lent out, the librarian does a quick inspection to check for damage." I poked a finger at the broken spine. "The damage to this book is severe and very visible. The librarian would have noticed it and sent the book for repair and wouldn't have allowed you to take it out."

"It was like that when I borrowed it." She was sticking to her story.

"I'm sorry, it wasn't." I opened the book to one of the large stains. "You borrowed this book over a month ago. This stain is still wet. I'd say it happened a couple of days ago at the latest."

Mrs Thompson said nothing.

"The book is beyond repair. And large-print books are expensive."

"I ain't payin' for somethin' I didn't do."

"That's up to you. But if you refuse to pay, we will have no choice but to rescind your borrower's ticket."

"What the fuck does that mean? Speak bleedin' English."

"It means you won't be allowed to take out any more books," Sally said, sliding Mrs Thompson's file over the counter to me.

"I don't care. I ain't payin'."

"The debt will go on to the Council's records." To make it even clearer to the woman I said, "This means that, for instance, if you ever wanted to move to another Council house, you would have to pay off the debt before the Housing Department would move you."

"Bleedin' 'ell, that's ridiculous! All for a poxy library book."

"That's the rule."

"I've got my name down for one of them big houses on King Street, I'm almost at the top of the list."

I didn't say anything. The ball was in Mrs Thompson's court.

"How much?" she asked, sighing.

"I don't know. I'll have to look up the cost. I'll write to you with the details."

"That'll fuckin' 'ave to do, then." She shuffled off, muttering about the unfairness of life.

I made a note in Mrs Thompson's folder, temporarily stopping her borrower's ticket. I also determined to fill out an incident report, putting on record Mrs Thompson's unacceptable language. That way, other Council officials would be made aware of her behaviour.

Sally thanked me for intervening. "I didn't know it would stop her from moving house."

"The Housing Department probably would overlook such a debt, but when I saw where she was living now, I thought it likely that she'd be on the waiting list to move out, so I used the threat as a lever to get her to cough up."

"It worked."

"Let's hope so. I'd better go and start the paperwork. At

times I wish I was back in your shoes. It seems that every time someone so much as blows their nose in here, I have to fill out a form in triplicate for the town hall."

Sally laughed.

As I was approaching my office, I heard the phone ringing. I quickened my step to try to catch it before it stopped.

"Senior Librarian," I breathed out.

"Sorry, did I make you run?" Gillian said.

"I was coming up the stairs when I heard the phone ring."

"I was beginning to think you were on your break or something."

"No, no, just sorting out something downstairs."

"I'm calling about your missing tramp. I'm sorry, Simon, but the news isn't good."

I dropped into my chair, my stomach beginning to knot; I could guess what was coming next.

"A body was found on Friday in the disused Cricket pavilion. From the papers that were found on him, it seems likely it was your Fred. He'd been there for a few days."

"Oh, no," I said quietly.

"Sorry it isn't better news."

"No." I rubbed my nose. "Thanks for getting back to me."

"There will have to be a post mortem of course, but I don't think they suspect foul play."

"No, he'll have gone in there to get out of the cold I suppose, and just passed away. Leastways that's what I hope."

"You're probably right."

We chatted for a couple more minutes before Gill told me she had to attend a meeting. "Now you're not going to leave it as long before contacting me again, are you?"

"No, Auntie Gill, I'll come round and see you sometime soon."

"Good boy," she said as she rang off.

I put my head in my hands and sighed. "Poor Fred."

Sitting up, I saw that it was almost lunchtime, so I decided to knock off a couple of minutes early. Often Mark would make me some sandwiches. Although I liked seeing him at lunchtime in the café, he was always run off his feet, it being his busiest time. Eating out all the time wasn't cheap either. But we'd decided I'd pop in today.

It wasn't as busy in the café as I'd thought. There was a group of teenage girls in school uniform at a table in the corner. They giggled every time Mark went near them. I smiled to myself. Hands off, girls, he's mine, I thought, taking a table as far from the schoolgirls as I could.

Mark soon came over, notepad in hand.

"I see your fan club is in this afternoon," I said, smiling.

He blushed. "They're getting to be a pain."

"The price of beauty."

"Shut up. What do you want?"

I raised an eyebrow. "I hope you don't talk to the other patrons that way."

Mark leaned down and spoke in my ear. "Only the ones I'm in love with."

I wanted so much to take him into my arms and kiss him at that moment. "I love you, too," I said quietly.

He smiled. I gave him my order, and he went into the back to fix it.

"You chatting up the waiter?" Mary said quietly once she'd sat down opposite.

"Don't need to," I smiled.

She just shook her head. Although we hadn't planned to eat together, we often did. And it would give me an opportunity to tell her about Fred.

I put a hand on top of hers and spoke softly. "I'm afraid I've got some bad news."

She smiled. "Stop messing about."

"It's about Fred."

Her face fell as I began telling her what I knew.

"Oh, no!" She got out a handkerchief and rubbed at her nose.

"I think he'd have been in his late sixties, not an old age

normally, but considering his lifestyle, I imagine his body had just had enough."

Mark came back with my food and took Mary's order. He noticed she wasn't her usual bright and breezy self, so I filled him in.

"You ought to go to the funeral," he said. "Assuming there is one."

"I'll find out. If there is a service I don't suppose many people will show up."

Mary indicated she wanted to go, too.

"LUUUUUCY, I'M HOOOOOOME!" I shouted out as usual when I came in later that evening.

Mark came from the kitchen. "Did you have a good day despite the news about Fred?"

I sighed. "Not really, I'll tell you all about it over dinner."

"Okay." He hesitated. "It's almost ready."

I'd given up trying to convince him that he didn't have to cook after spending all day in the café; he always brushed aside my worries.

"Daphne had some steak and kidney pie left over, so I just boiled a few potatoes and vegetables to go with it," Mark said, putting the food on the table.

"Looks great as ever," I said, tucking in.

Dinner was quiet. We each spoke a little about our day, but I was distracted and Mark knew it.

I'd just put the plates in the sink when Mark asked, "So, what happened to upset you at work?"

I sat back at the table and took his hand in mine. I told him about Auntie Gillian, and the conversation I'd had with her.

"I felt awful when I brushed away her comments about 'finding a nice girl.' I should have told her about you." I squeezed his hand. "I felt like somehow I'd denied your love for me. I'm sorry."

"Don't be silly," he said, hugging me. "I understand."

"I'm going to put it right, though," I said, feeling a new sense of determination. "I'm going to invite her round this Friday, if that's all right with you?"

Mark nodded.

"And if she can't accept who I am, then that's her loss."

"Are you sure? She obviously meant a great deal to you when you were little."

"Yes, and she still does, but she has to know the sort of person I am. Mark, you've made me the happiest guy alive. If someone asks me a direct question in future, unless I'd be in physical danger by revealing my secret, I'm going to tell them I'm gay. I won't out you as well."

"Thanks." He kissed my cheek. "But if it's someone you've known for a long time, I don't mind them knowing about me."

"You're the greatest," I said kissing him on the lips.

We heard someone knocking at the front door. Answering it, I saw it was Paul.

"I'm not disturbing you two, am I?" he asked, stepping inside.

"Not at all," Mark said as he came in from the kitchen. "You've just delayed Simon from doing the washing up."

Paul smiled. "You ought to get a machine. Helen wouldn't be without ours. In fact, I think she'd get rid of me before parting with that dishwasher."

We smiled. Then Mark offered him a cup of tea, which he declined.

I gestured to the armchair and Paul sat.

"Mark, I'm sorry if we upset you with our questions yesterday about how you two met."

"It's all right." Mark came and sat next to me on the sofa and took my hand. "A few things in my past weren't very nice, and I'm not very proud of them."

Paul's face was a mixture of concern and puzzlement. Mark took a deep breath and looked over at me. I'd previously told him he didn't have to reveal his past to anyone, as it wasn't any of their business, but he'd talked about how he didn't want to have any secrets from his friends and how something like that could come up one day, and he'd rather have his friends hear it from him rather than some gossipmonger.

I smiled and gave his hand a squeeze of reassurance.

"You might not like this, but I think of you as a friend."

Paul sat forward. "If it's too painful, I understand."

"No." Mark shook his head. "You should know, I'm just afraid of your reaction and what you might do."

Paul's puzzlement increased. "I can't think that anything you've done could change my opinion of you."

Mark began to tell his story, starting with the death of his mother and his father's attitude towards him, then went on to describe his father's discovering him with his friend Danny. When Mark related the details of his father's behaviour, Paul shook his head.

Mark ploughed bravely on. I put an arm around him when he started talking about his time working on the streets. Paul showed momentary surprise, but it was soon replaced with his usual concerned expression.

Paul was further surprised when he learned I had been one of Mark's clients. Mark spoke about how he'd hurt his hands, and me springing him from the hospital.

"Well," Paul shook his head, "I don't mind admitting I'm surprised, I had no idea. I'm sorry. I can't begin to imagine the horrible things that you've faced. But I don't know why you'd think I'd be angry?"

"Sam. I thought you might not like him being near someone who did what I had to."

"Com'ere." Paul got to his feet and opened his arms.

Mark stood and walked into the embrace.

"I've never thought you and Simon's relationship with Sam was anything other than...proper. Sam never stops talking about you two. And it's always good."

"Thanks," Mark said, slapping Paul on the back before

withdrawing.

"Hey, Paul," I said, trying to lighten the mood. "With you hugging another bloke, you don't want to come and play for our team, do you?"

It took him a second to process this, then he tipped his head back and laughed. "You daft sod. I'll stick to women, or rather one woman."

"Probably for the best," Mark said. "A hunk like you would mean I'd have competition where Simon was concerned."

Paul reddened.

"You're more than enough hunk for me," I said, squeezing Mark's shoulder. Feeling giddy with relief that Paul had taken the news of Mark's past so well, I opened my mouth and said something I shouldn't. "But I've always had a thing for men in hardhats."

Paul shook his head, his blush increasing. The man was a builder and we regularly saw him walking around with a white hardhat on his head.

"Sorry, Paul." I was already regretting my admission.

"No problem." Paul changed the subject, a fact for which I was grateful. "What you said earlier. Sam, he can come round here whenever he wants, that will never change. Besides, my life wouldn't be worth living if I ever tried to stop him." He chuckled.

"Thanks, Paul," Mark and I said at the same time.

"I mean it. Before you two started to be a regular part of his life, Sam was shy, quiet, didn't seem to have much of a spark about him. Now," he grinned. "We can't shut him up."

We laughed.

Once Paul had left, I gave Mark a hug. "Feel better now?"

Mark nodded. "I thought he'd be all right about it. I imagine he'll tell Helen. Not sure about Sam, though."

I shook my head. I thought it unlikely he'd tell Sam.

"Maybe we'll wait a few years until he's older."

Sam was pretty mature for his age, but this was stuff he didn't need to deal with just yet.

"There's just your Gran left to tell now."

"I know she'll be fine about it"

Mark smiled. "It seems to get a bit easier each time."

MARK REMEMBERED MY penchant for men in hard hats. He came into the bedroom about a week after our talk with Paul, naked apart from a canvas tool belt around his waist, a hard hat on his head, and a lascivious smile on his face. "Heard you had a job for me, sir."

"I do? Oh, yes, I do!" I tackled Mark to the bed and began to lick him in all his exposed places, and there were plenty.

"Condom," Mark gasped when I engulfed him.

I hated that we had to play it safe. It took the spontaneity out of making love, but it was a fact of life, and one Mark insisted on. I hated the taste of rubber, but it was either that or no blowing Mark. Because I was a virgin when Mark and I got together, he wasn't as strict about me wearing protection when he went down on me. This usually resulted in me getting an unfair share of loving. However, I was determined to reward Mark for getting hold of a hardhat and a tool belt. Reaching over to the bedside table I yanked open the drawer; it came out and spilled its contents over the bedroom carpet.

"Shit!"

Mark laughed.

"Don't move," I said, getting off the bed and retrieving one of the foil packets. The cleanup of the other items could wait, but I couldn't.

"Now, where was I?"

"About to play a game of poker?" Mark suggested.

"Ha, ha."

I tore the foil with my teeth and extracted the latex disc. We'd gotten hold of a porn video a month or so before. I'd been impressed at how one of the actors had ripped open the packet, put the condom in his mouth, and used his lips to put the rubber on. I'd tried to emulate this a few times but either ended up biting into the condom or Mark, and on one memorable occasion almost swallowing the darned rubber.

So I used my hands, one to hold Mark's beautiful erect dick, the other to roll the rubber down said beautiful erect dick. I kissed the head then sat back on my ankles to admire the view.

"Simon!" Mark groaned.

Now I had my prize in sight I felt able to wait, but evidently Mark didn't. Taking pity on my lover, I stuck out my tongue and washed it around the head of Mark's dick, causing him to moan.

The dick, like the rest of Mark, was a thing of beauty. For some time after Mark and I had gotten together I'm ashamed to say my blowjobs were inadequate. Mark had reassured me he enjoyed whatever I did to him. Thankfully, frequent practice had improved my skills and although I knew I'd never be as good as Mark, if his current moans were any indication, I was doing enough to bring him pleasure.

Deciding I'd had my fill of the taste of rubber, I moved down to lick his balls. Until Mark, I had no idea being licked down there could feel so amazing. But then there was so much I didn't know before Mark.

"Oh, Simon," Mark groaned.

And if having his balls played with was good, then making love to his bottom with my tongue should tip him over.

"Oh, hell!"

I feared the neighbours would complain about the noise, so reluctantly I moved back to Mark's waiting phallus and took him down to the base in one long swallow.

"Simon!"

I guess that didn't work, I thought, hoping next door wouldn't bang on the wall with a shoe. He did once when Mark and I had really gotten into it.

"Please, gotta, gotta."

I loved how Mark couldn't form sentences when he was

close. It never ceased to amaze me how someone as plain and ordinary as me could render a beautiful man like Mark almost speechless.

"Ahhh!"

I felt the rubber expand in my mouth, and Mark sank back against the covers.

"Oh, God," he panted. "Wait a minute and I'll—"

I leaned down and kissed him. "It's okay, take your time."

I didn't mind waiting. In fact a part of me liked bringing Mark pleasure without needing him to reciprocate. I didn't want to think about all the men he'd had to be with, but I bet none of them gave him pleasure without expecting something back in return. I liked to think I was making secret deposits in Mark's pleasure bank.

Chapter 7

THE REST OF the week passed with few problems. I'd found out the cost of replacing the damaged large-print book and sent the bill to Mrs Thompson. It remained to be seen if she would pay up.

Auntie Gill rang on Tuesday morning to tell me the pathologist's report showed the most likely cause of Fred's death was heart failure. She went on to say there would be a funeral service at the crematorium on Friday afternoon.

"Auntie, are you doing anything on Friday night?"

"No, dear, why?"

"I wondered if you wanted to come over for dinner. You're right, I haven't seen you in ages, and I'd like to have a talk with you as well."

"Thank you, that would be wonderful."

As I'd suspected, there were few mourners at Fred's funeral. The vicar, who obviously didn't know Fred, did his best, but with little material to work with, he could only speak in generalities. Apart from the Vicar's words and various readings from the Bible, including the congregation's reciting the twenty-third Psalm, the service was over in less than fifteen minutes.

Although the funerals at the crem were always conducted with all due dignity, I couldn't help thinking they were like a production line. You entered the crematorium through one door, at the back, then waited in a little foyer until the doors to the main room were opened. Then you took your seat for the service. Once this was over, you shook the minister's hand and walked out through the front door into the garden of remembrance. You could see the mourners for the next funeral lining up to gain admittance through the back door. I think they could get through three funerals per hour. Dignified, but efficient.

After shaking the Vicar's proffered hand, Mary and I went into the garden; we'd bought a small bouquet of flowers, the only ones Fred had received.

"Mr Peters?" a man in his mid-forties and wearing a business suit asked. I had forgotten to take off my name badge.

"Yes?"

"I'm Thomas Anderson from Smith, Temple and Jones. The solicitors on West Street?"

I nodded.

"Forgive me for introducing myself at such a…a time as this, but would you, or someone from the library, be able to visit our offices sometime in the near future?"

"I suppose so. But why?"

"Mr Jones left a will and we need to speak to someone from the library about its contents."

I was puzzled that Fred would have left a will and that the library was mentioned in it. "When I get back to the office on

Monday I'll give you a ring to arrange an appointment, would that be all right?"

"Thank you, and once again, I apologise for the intrusion."

After he'd gone, Mary spoke up. "Wow, that's a surprise."

"Just what I was thinking," I admitted.

There was little for me to do back at the office, so I spent the time worrying about Auntie Gill's visit. I had no reason to think she was homophobic, as I'd said to Mark; I simply didn't want to disappoint her. She'd been an important part of my early life.

I GREW INCREASINGLY agitated as the time got closer to Auntie Gill's arrival.

"Calm down," Mark soothed a number of times.

"Sorry. It's just…" I didn't know how to put my feelings into words. "I'd like her to give me…us, her blessing."

"Is there any reason why she won't? I mean, has she ever shown any sign of being homophobic?"

"No, but I don't think the subject has ever come up."

"It's almost seven now, so you'll soon be put out of your misery," Mark said, giving me a quick kiss on the lips.

I heard a car door close, so I peeked through the curtains. "She's here." I nervously smoothed my hands down the shirt I'd changed into after getting home from work.

"You'll be fine. Always remember, I love you," Mark said just before I opened the door.

"You should have said you were having a friend round, I could have come another time," Gill said once she'd situated herself on the sofa.

I guessed this was as good a time as any to spill the beans. I certainly wasn't going to deny my relationship with Mark a second time.

"Auntie Gill," I said, coming to sit next to her. "You remember when we talked on Monday, and you told me it was about time I settled down with someone?" I knew she'd actually said "settle down with a nice girl," but it was near enough.

"Yes, I remember." She smiled at me.

"Well," I took a deep breath. "There's no easy way of telling you this, and the last thing I want to do is to disappoint you, but Auntie, I have settled down with someone. Mark and I live together."

"I knew it!" She smiled and clapped her hands. "The old saying is true, it takes one to know one."

"Huh?" I didn't understand.

"The moment I walked through the door, I could sense there was something between you two."

"Oh, right, but how? I mean, we weren't kissing or anything, and I don't follow the bit about it taking one to know one."

"I'm a lesbian!"

"Huh?" I said again.

"Simon, close your mouth, otherwise something might fly into it."

"You? You? I never had the slightest idea."

She smiled. "I don't go around advertising the fact. But think about it, I never got married."

"Yes, but that didn't mean I'd jump to the conclusion you were a lesbian."

"True. I've been in a relationship for about five years now. We don't live together, unfortunately...my partner has to look after her sick mother, and that's almost a full-time job."

"I see. Sorry, I've been panicking all day wondering what your reaction would be, and all along you're like us." Relief flooded through me.

Mark moved from the chair to sit next to me on the sofa.

Gill and I chatted for a while until she said, "Well, this is all very nice, but I'm hungry, and you promised to feed me."

"Whoops," Mark said. "I've got a casserole in the oven. It should be ready to serve now."

"And he cooks, too." Auntie Gill grinned.

The three of us had a great time over dinner. Gill was delighted to give Mark details concerning the more embarrassing episodes of my childhood.

"I knew it was a mistake to invite you round here," I said after one particularly face-reddening story involving me, a bunch of keys and the storm grate at the corner of our street.

"You were a joy to look after."

"Do you still carry a small bag of sweets in your handbag?" Mark asked.

"No, not anymore." Gill admitted. "I've no more special little boys to spoil," she said, pinching one of my cheeks.

This caused Mark and Gill to laugh.

"So, tell me about the lady in your life," Mark asked, bringing out a cheesecake for dessert.

"She's called Mandy. She has a part-time job in the typing pool at Social Services. But as I said, she has to look after her mother most of the time. Her mother has Alzheimer's. A carer comes in every morning so Mandy is free to work. She can usually get someone to sit with her mother on a Friday or Saturday night, so that's when we generally go out."

I nodded.

"I suppose it's easier for two women to be seen together than it is for two men. But sometimes I wish we could just go out and be ourselves. We both hate the idea of a gay nightclub, that's just not our scene."

"The King George!" Both Mark and I said at the same time. We looked at each other and laughed.

"What's that?"

I told her, then looked over at Mark. I didn't need to verbalise my question. We'd grown so used to one another, we could often communicate without words.

He nodded and smiled.

"How would you like to go to the pub tomorrow, Auntie? We could take you both."

"I'd have to ring Mandy, but I can't see why not. I know she's got someone to look after Mabel tomorrow night."

"Do you think Tim plays there on a Saturday night, too?" I asked Mark while Auntie Gill was in the next room using the phone.

"No idea; I'll ring Tom and Cliff to find out. I guess you'd want me to sing again if Tim is playing?"

"It's up to you." I really wanted to hear my man sing again, but I knew he didn't want to do it too often.

He smiled. "Yeah, why not. Though it all depends on Tim."

"You'll knock 'em dead," I said as Gill came back into the room.

"Mandy would love to go out with you two, and what's this about Mark knocking people dead?"

Mark nodded at me to tell her.

"Apart from being gorgeous and a wonderful cook, Mark also has the singing voice of an angel."

Mark blushed again.

Gill chuckled. "And will you sing for us tomorrow night?"

"It all depends if the pianist is on tomorrow. I'll just ring and find out."

Mark got up and went into the other room.

"Where did you two meet?" Gill asked.

"We bumped into each other in the street and just got talking." I didn't want to go into all that again. Fortunately Gill didn't ask any more questions.

"And how long have you known each other?"

"We first met just over a year ago…and we told each other that we loved one another on Christmas Day."

"That's great!"

"Christmas is just one of our anniversaries."

She raised an eyebrow.

"Yeah, Mark actually got down on one knee on the beach and proposed to me when we were on holiday in Menorca last August."

I showed her the ring.

"So romantic," she bubbled. "Of course, you both wear similar rings. I hadn't made the connection."

"I know. Honestly, Auntie, I'm the luckiest bloke alive."

"No he isn't, that's me," Mark said coming back into the kitchen. "There was no reply at Tom and Cliff's, so I rang Tim. I just caught him before he left for the George. He said he doesn't normally play on a Saturday."

My face fell. "Oh well, we'll still have a nice time."

"But as I agreed to sing, Tim said he'll play tomorrow, too. He said we went down a storm last time, and everyone's been asking him when I was going to sing again."

"See. I told you that you were a hit."

Mark smiled. "Tim said he'd make an announcement tonight at the pub. He thinks the place will be extra full tomorrow. I think he's exaggerating."

"He's so modest," I told Gill, getting up and kissing Mark's cheek.

Mark shook his head. "Tim wants us to go over to his place tomorrow afternoon so we can run through a few numbers in advance. Would that be a problem?"

"Mandy won't be able to get someone to sit with her mother for that long," Gill said.

I was depressed that my plans weren't coming out as I'd hoped.

"If we give you directions, would you be able to get there under your own steam?" Mark asked.

"That would be fine."

Going back into the other room, Mark called out, "I just might be able to catch Tim before he goes; he said he'd hang on for a few minutes."

I got up and put the kettle on. I'd remembered that Gill preferred tea rather than coffee.

"That's all settled," Mark said a few minutes later when he came back into the kitchen. "We're to be at Tim's by three-thirty tomorrow."

"Sam won't be pleased we're going out without him again," I said, pouring the tea.

"Who's Sam?" Gill asked, accepting her cup.

I'd just started to tell her when I heard the front door open and close.

"You two in the kitchen?"

"Yes, and—" I started to say.

"Hope you're not doing each other at the sink or anything gross like...Oh!" Sam froze in place at the kitchen door.

"You must be Sam," Gill said in her best schoolteacher voice.

"Um, uh, yeah, that's me."

I didn't know whether to laugh or be angry. Fortunately, Mark spoke up and saved me from having to decide.

"It's okay. Don't worry." Mark pulled back a chair. "Come, sit, you look as though you need to."

"Uh, yeah, thanks. Sorry."

Mark put a hand on Sam's shoulder. "This is Simon's Aunt Gillian."

"Hello," Sam said, sounding unusually shy. Turning to Mark and me, he continued, "I didn't know, I'm sorry."

"It's all right. I already knew about Simon and Mark," Gillian told him. "Now, would you like a cup of tea, or some of that awful coffee stuff Simon and Mark insist on drinking?"

Sam smiled and visibly relaxed. "Tea's fine, thanks."

Mark got up and brought another cup and saucer to the table.

"Posh," Sam said. "Normally I just get offered a mug."

"Watch it," I said. "You're not out of the woods yet, young man."

"Sorry." Sam dipped his head. "I remembered what you said in Menorca about not revealing personal stuff, but I didn't know you had company"

I reached over and patted his shoulder. "It's fine. Like you said, you weren't to know."

"Thanks." Sam's smile started to return. "Got any biscuits?"

"What brought you over here anyway?" Mark asked, getting

up to retrieve the packet of digestives.

"Me and Billy, we, uh…He didn't complete his sentence, obviously not wanting to out himself in front of Gill.

"It's all right, remember what I said about how Auntie Gill is okay about Mark and me?"

"Well." Sam took a drink of his tea then a huge bite out of his biscuit. I was pleased to see that he didn't dunk the latter into the former. "Simon and Mark sometimes let me and my boyfriend, Billy, sleep in their spare room. Both of us only have single beds in our houses, you see."

"And your parents don't mind you two staying the night together?" Gill asked.

"Mine are fine about it. Billy was a bit scared about telling his olds that he was gay, but when they found out, they were okay with it, too."

"I'm sure my mum and dad wouldn't have accepted me loving another woman, much less countenancing me sleeping with her in the same bed." She shook her head. "But I suppose times change."

Sam nodded.

Mark looked at me and I nodded my agreement.

"Okay, seeing as you asked so nicely, you and Billy can stay." Mark told him.

"Thanks." Sam stood and headed for the door. "I'll go get him."

"He's full of beans," Gill said when Sam had raced out of the house.

We agreed, although I couldn't help remembering what Paul had said about how Sam used to be shy and withdrawn.

A moment or two later, a grinning Sam and Billy arrived.

"Thanks for letting us stay again," Billy said.

"You're welcome," I told him.

Gill checked her watch and said she should be going. "But first, I'll give you a hand clearing up."

"No, it's okay, Sam and Billy can do it," I said. Raising a

hand to quell Sam's protest, I added, "in payment for staying here tonight."

❖

SHAKING MARK AWAKE the next morning, I said, "I think we ought to get up."

"No. Go back to sleep," Mark mumbled. "Don't have to work at the weekend anymore, remember?"

This was true. Daphne had set on a number of youth trainees. They didn't get paid terribly well, but could earn more in tips. For Mark it meant he had his weekends to himself.

"No." I shook Mark's shoulder. "It's the boys. From the smell of it I think they're cooking us breakfast."

"Why didn't you say so earlier?" Mark asked, sounding much more awake.

We dressed, used the bathroom, and went downstairs.

"We woke about half an hour ago and were hungry," Sam said when Mark asked him why he'd made breakfast for us.

"Typical teenagers, always hungry," Mark grinned.

"How many teenagers cook breakfast for their honorary dads?" Sam fired back.

"He's got you there," I told Mark.

But evidently Mark wasn't giving up so easily. "We'll have to go to the supermarket early next week. Those two are eating us out of house and home." He pointed his fork over at the boys, who were grinning around mouthfuls of scrambled egg.

After swallowing, Sam asked, "Do you two still have a Chinese takeaway on Thursday nights?"

"Usually," Mark said. "It's something I used to do when I was at home, and Simon agreed to carry on the tradition."

"We'll have to invite ourselves round some time," Sam told Billy.

"Cheeky buggers. I'm sure your parents would feed you," I said.

"Yeah, but they don't have Chinese very often," Sam admitted.

"We'll see," Mark said. "I don't want your parents to think we're monopolising you both."

"They wouldn't think that," Sam said.

"Even so, I'm sure they like seeing you at home some of the time, and as it's your exam year and…" I ground to a halt, knowing I was going all librarian on him.

"They all know that if we come here you'll make us study," Billy said.

"Which reminds me, have you got any homework due?" I asked, unable to stop myself.

WITH THE BOYS at Billy's house, Mark and I spent the next few hours cleaning. Then Mark pottered around the garden, doing whatever it is people do in gardens. After that we both took a bath in preparation for going out to the George.

Once bathed, I went into the bedroom to see what clothes I could put on. I cared little about what I wore, but I wanted to look nice for Mark's sake. He was wearing a pair of tight, cream-coloured trousers with a midnight blue shirt and a white T-shirt underneath. He looked gorgeous in anything, or even nothing at all, but he looked especially wonderful in those clothes.

"I've changed my mind," I said after giving Mark a long, slow up and down.

"About what?"

"I want to rip off your sexy clothes and make mad passionate love to you for the rest of the day."

He gave me a chaste kiss. "That'll have to keep you going until tonight."

"Tease!" I said, pouting.

WE MADE GOOD time to Tim's house. I'd driven over there,

but Mark insisted he'd drive back.

"For the first time you're going to be able to have a drink when we go out somewhere, and besides, I think staying off the alcohol will help my voice."

"If you're sure," I shrugged, not that bothered about sticking to soft drinks.

We'd barely gotten out of the car before the front door opened and a smiling Tim was coming to greet us.

"It's great to see you both again," he said.

"Glad to see you, too," I replied.

We were ushered into the house. It was cluttered but scrupulously clean. There were paintings hung on every wall, and in the back room, the one that held Tim's upright piano, there was a whole wall of shelving containing books, LPs, CDs and musical scores. Photo frames with a younger and happy-looking Tim with another, slightly taller, man covered every available surface. I assumed the other man was Tim's late partner, Doug.

"Forgive my manners, would you two like a cup of tea?"

"We'd prefer coffee, if you have it?" Mark asked.

"Of course. I keep a jar of instant for visitors."

He bustled off into the kitchen, Mark following a few moments later to offer his assistance.

"Gracious, no." I could hear Tim say. "I'll be through in a minute, and this kitchen is too small for two to work in comfortably."

Mark came back into the room and sat next to me on a two-seater sofa.

Tim entered a few minutes later carrying a huge tray which not only contained the expected tea and coffee things, but also a large selection of cakes, scones, and pastries.

"Knowing you were coming, I did a bit of baking. Dougie always used to say I went overboard when I baked."

He looked wistfully over at one of the framed photographs. It showed two happy young men, arms around one another, gazing deeply into each other's eyes.

"Thank you," Mark told him, accepting the tray and setting it on a coffee table. "It all looks delicious. Simon and I haven't eaten since breakfast."

"Oh, I hope there's enough, I might have time to whip up some—"

"No, please," I said, stopping Tim from getting to his feet. "There's more than enough here. Mark's right, it looks delicious, I don't know where to start."

Tim smiled and relaxed.

I was complimenting Tim on the lightness of his pastry when there was a knock at the door.

"I completely forgot. That'll be Tom and Cliff." Tim shot up and headed towards the hallway. "They said they'd take you out, Simon, while Mark and I run through a few songs."

I'd been looking forward to hearing Mark practice, but knew I'd also enjoy spending time with Tom and Cliff.

"Come in. We're in the music room," Tim said in the hallway.

"Hello," Cliff said, walking towards us with his arms open.

We both stood and hugged him.

"Do I get one, too?" Tom asked, appearing in—and almost filling—the doorway.

I obliged.

"And we hear you're going to sing again, Mark. That's great," Tom said, letting go his huge hold on me and advancing on Mark.

Mark explained that my Auntie Gill and her partner were coming over tonight, and that was the main reason why we were making the trip.

"Excellent!" Cliff said. "We don't see enough lesbian couples at the George. I think they believe it's just for men, but everyone, gay, straight, lesbian, or bisexual is welcome."

"Shall we go into the front room?" Tim asked. "There aren't enough chairs in here for everyone. Oh, gosh, I haven't had as many visitors in such a long time."

I could tell Tim was in his element, fussing round everyone, getting them drinks and fretting about whether he'd baked enough scones.

"Tim, it's okay," Cliff eventually said. "There's plenty of food—I fed the human dustbin before we came out." He pointed to a grinning Tom.

"I've still got room for a couple of your cakes," Tom said.

"I've no doubt about that." Cliff smiled.

"I'm a growing lad," Tom told him.

We all sympathised with him.

Once we'd had our fill of Tim's excellent baking, Tom and Cliff said that we might as well get going.

"We thought we'd leave a visit to the centre of York till Mark was with us," Cliff said as we drove away from Tim's.

"Thanks, I'm sure he'd like to see the Minster and everything. I'd like to bring Sam and Billy, too, if that's all right?"

"Of course it's all right," Tom said. "How is my little mate?"

"Cheeky as ever," I smiled.

We drove around a few of the nearby villages—each seeming prettier than the previous one. I mentioned this to the guys.

"You're right. We're lucky to live round here, but unfortunately the locals can't live off the view," Cliff said, turning round in the front passenger seat to address me. "Rural unemployment is very high, and it's next to impossible for them to be able to buy affordable housing in their communities."

"I hadn't thought of that," I admitted.

"And what property that does come onto the market gets snapped up at a highly inflated price by southerners who want a second home," Cliff added with an edge of bitterness. "Sorry, it's another of my soapbox topics."

"That's all right." I was surprised at how passionate he was on the subject.

"Now you've seen most of what there is, we might as well head back to our place for a bit," Tom said.

❖

BY THE TIME we set off for the King George, I was nervous for Mark's sake. I couldn't explain why; he had a wonderful voice, and if the reaction was half as good as last time, I knew all would be well.

"Stop worrying," Tom told me.

"I know. I'm being silly."

"Yes you are. He's a big boy."

I laughed, hoping it didn't sound hollow. I was trying to put on a front for the others, but inwardly I was worried, and I was angry at myself for being so pathetic.

Mark wasn't at the pub when we entered. I must have looked concerned.

"He'll still be at Tim's," Cliff said. "We'll save some seats for them and your aunt and her friend. If you remember from last time, Tim doesn't come until it's almost time for him to play."

"I remember," I said.

"I think you could do with a large drink." Tom smiled at me.

"Go on then, Mark's driving home, I'll have a double gin and tonic."

"Good man." Tom turned to the bar and got Gary's attention.

"You're Mark's partner, aren't you?" Gary asked me.

"That's right," I nodded, feeling really happy that someone whom I barely knew was acknowledging that Mark and I were a couple.

"When Tim announced Mark would be singing tonight, there was a bit of excitement in the place. Folks remember his performance. I've lost count of the number of people who've come up and asked me when he was going to sing again."

My chest puffed up with pride for my man.

We got our drinks and sat at the same table we'd had on our previous visit.

Glancing over at the door, checking for Mark's arrival, I saw Auntie Gill come in with another woman just behind her. They got their drinks at the bar, then I waved them over to our table.

"You found the place okay?" I asked once all the introductions had been made.

"Quite easily, thanks," Mandy said. "Though it's a bit too far to come every week."

I had to agree with them on that.

"Mark not here yet?" Gill asked.

"He'll come with the pianist later," I said. "They've spent the afternoon practising."

After the large amount of food I'd packed away at Tim's, I only wanted a sandwich. I ordered one for Mark, too. I wasn't sure if he'd want anything, but was certain it wouldn't go to waste with Tom around.

Finally, after the place had almost filled to capacity, the entertainment walked in to a smattering of applause. Gary broke off from the order he was filling and served Mark and Tim instead. Drinks in hand, they made their way over to the seats Tom had had to guard quite fiercely.

"If you hadn't turned up soon, Simon would have had a nervous breakdown. It's a wonder he has any fingernails left." Tom laughed at my sheepish expression.

"Missed me?"

Mark leaned over and kissed me on the lips. It was great to be able to show affection in public.

"No, I was just wondering if I could score a date with Gary," I looked over at the sexy barman.

"He'll have to come through me first," Mark said, flexing his muscles.

Tim told us he and Mark would perform a few numbers together. Then he would play on his own for a while, to allow Mark's voice to rest. Then, after Tim's break, the two would perform in tandem for a last set.

The crowd hushed as soon as Tim began his introduction to the first song, "Embraceable You." I noticed quite a few people had smiles on their faces when Mark started to sing. I glanced over at Gill and Mandy; their expressions were a mixture of surprise and amazement. I couldn't help my smile of pride in my man as his rich baritone filled the room.

They received a much-deserved round of applause once the song finished.

Tim and Mark went on to perform several more numbers, mostly from Broadway or West End shows, the attentive audience greeting each one with enthusiasm.

"And for my last number before my break," Mark said. "I would like to perform a song from Rodgers and Hammerstein's *South Pacific.*"

"Oh, shit!" I said quietly.

I didn't think I could cope with him singing it again.

Gill looked curiously at me. However, I sighed with relief when Tim began to play "Some Enchanted Evening."

When the applause died down, Mark stepped off the stage and began to make his way to our table, shaking a few hands and, from the looks of things, receiving more than a few pleasant comments from his appreciative audience. I felt emboldened enough to stand up, embrace him, and give him a quick kiss.

"You were magnificent!" I told him.

"Thanks." Mark dipped his head. "The practice at Tim's earlier really helped."

"I noticed that you didn't need to look down at the words very often," Tom said, clapping a hand on Mark's shoulder.

One of the waitresses brought over a drink for Mark.

"It's on the house," she said.

It was non-alcoholic, so Mark accepted it gratefully.

Once Tim finished his solo spot he began to weave his way through the tables toward us. A few people stopped him, one or two pointing in Mark's direction.

The same waitress came back with a tomato juice for Tim.

"We seem to be a hit," Tim toasted Mark with his glass.

"I know. I'm amazed." Mark replied.

"Nonsense, you've got a beautiful voice."

As people went to the bar, they patted Mark and or Tim on the shoulder as they passed.

"Mark, I better get your autograph before you start charging," Tom said.

We laughed.

Mark picked at his sandwich. "I don't feel like eating much, I've still got a few butterflies."

"You sang after eating a whole meal last time," Tom pointed out.

"I didn't know I was going to sing beforehand."

About half an hour later Tim and Mark made their way back onto the stage.

"Ladies and gentlemen," Mark said. "I'm originally from Newcastle, and so I had to include a song from the northeast. I'm sure it'll be familiar to you all." Turning to Tim, he said, "Maestro?"

Tim nodded and Mark began to sing.

I smiled; my man was obviously feeling much more comfortable about performing.

I remembered *When the Boat Comes In* as the theme song from the TV show of the same name. I'd never heard Mark speak—let alone sing—in such a thick accent as he sang about how the boy would receive all kinds of fishes when the boat came in.

"Thank you," Mark said when he'd finished and received polite applause. "I've been adopted as an honorary Yorkshireman, so I'd like to sing "On Ilkla Moor Baht'at." But, alas, I had to ask Tim what *baht'at* meant. Of course I now know it's 'without a hat'. Please join in the chorus if you like."

The song was greeted with applause, and many took up Mark's invitation and joined in on the chorus.

Tim and Mark returned to their traditional repertoire for the remainder of the evening. I remembered Tim's comments from our last visit about how conservative the crowd was.

"For our finale tonight," Mark said, "I'm returning to *South Pacific.*"

Oh, no, I thought.

"I'm probably going to get lynched later for singing this.

The last time I performed it, I asked Simon to marry me."

The audience clapped and a few wolf whistled.

Oh, shit. I covered my face, uncomfortable with the attention.

"Fortunately, he said yes," Mark said just as Tim began to play the long introduction to "Younger than Springtime."

I braced myself, remembering what an emotional mess I'd been when Mark had sung it in Menorca.

"You are not going to cry, you are not going to cry," I repeated under my breath.

I hadn't been able to listen to the song since that amazing, unforgettable night, the night my beautiful Mark proposed to me on the beach.

I looked over at the people sitting near me. Tom and Cliff had moved closer together, Cliff's head resting on Tom's broad shoulder. Gill and Mandy were holding hands.

However, once Mark launched into the chorus, my resolve not to cry crumbled.

"Shit!" I said quietly, wiping at my eyes and blowing my nose.

When Mark stopped singing, and Tim had struck the last note, there was absolute silence in the room for a heartbeat before the place exploded into loud applause.

Chapter 8

IT WAS AFTER midnight by the time we got home from the George, so we fell straight into bed.

"Did you have a good time?" Mark asked, letting out a face-splitting yawn.

"The best. Thank you." I was still keyed up by it all. Mark, up on stage, singing to everyone, but it was me he came home with.

"Why're you thanking me?"

I kissed the back of his head. "For being you."

"Silly."

About a minute later I said, "I'm glad you sang 'Younger Than Springtime.' Despite making me cry, it was good to hear it again."

There was no reply.

"Mark. You awake?"

Still no answer.

I had a hard on and no boyfriend to help with it, so I rolled over and tried to will it down. After ten or fifteen minutes with no sign of my erection going away, I slid from under the covers and padded into the bathroom to take matters into my own hands.

As I got back into bed, Mark rolled toward me. "Where'd you go?" he asked sleepily.

"Nowhere." I smiled and kissed his cheek. "Go back to sleep."

"'Kay."

And within minutes he did just that. I lay awake a little longer, savouring my good fortune at being with such a wonderful and talented man.

"LOOKS LIKE OUR Sunday morning walk's off," Mark said after parting the bedroom curtains and looking out.

"Why?"

"It's chucking it down out there. Can't you hear it?"

Now he mentioned it, I could hear the rain tapping at the glass.

"Come back to bed." I yawned. "It's cold in here without you."

"Back in a minute." Mark left the room. A minute later I heard the toilet flush.

"Shit, you're freezing," I said, recoiling from Mark when he got under the covers.

"I think the heating's on the blink."

"Bugger! I'll go and thump the boiler later."

Mark chuckled. "I don't think that would help get it going."

"No, but it might help me."

I edged closer to him—he'd warmed up a little.

"Yuck, morning breath," he complained when I kissed him.

"Sorry." Mark's breath tasted minty; he must have brushed his teeth when he was in the bathroom.

I got up, wrapped a dressing gown around myself, and went

into the bathroom to take care of business.

"You're cold now," Mark said, once I'd gotten back into bed.

"Which would you have preferred? A cold bed partner or one with bad breath?" I snapped, feeling irritated that the heating wasn't working, and goodness knew when and how much it would cost to fix.

"C'mere." Mark wrapped his warm body around me, and my anger instantly drained away.

"Sorry."

He kissed my cheek. "It's okay."

I began to wonder, was this our first argument? Though did it qualify as such if only one party got angry? Mark and I had been a couple for ten months and I couldn't ever recall us having cross words. Was I dreaming? Had I been hit over the head last Christmas Eve and been in a coma ever since—Mark, and the wonderful life we'd built together, just hallucinations? If so, I hoped I would never wake up.

Eventually our hunger drove us into the coldness that was downstairs.

"Do you know much about gas boilers?" I asked, staring at the unresponsive heating equipment.

"Sorry. We were all electric at home."

"That must have been expensive." I turned a knob. But, yet again, nothing happened.

"And not that warm in the winter."

I slid the plastic panel closed before giving the front of the boiler a swift thump.

"Feel better now?" Mark asked.

"Not really." I flexed my sore fingers.

Mark chuckled, but he did kiss my fingers better.

"If we light the fire in the front room and put the oven on in here, at least we'll have a warm downstairs," Mark said.

"I knew there was a reason why I kept you around."

Mark shook his head. Going over to the cooker he lit the oven. "At least we have gas to the house, so it isn't lack of a gas supply."

"Right. I'll have to ring up an engineer tomorrow. Hope he can come out to have a look at it soon." This time I was determined not to get angry; it wasn't Mark's fault.

"Will you be able to get time off work to be in for the engineer?"

"I have a meeting tomorrow afternoon, but I think I'll be able to excuse myself from it if the guy says he can come that soon." I went into the front room to lay the fire.

❖

"DO WE NEED to go out anywhere today?" Mark asked.

We were standing at the kitchen sink, looking out over a soggy back garden.

"Don't think so." Then I remembered something. "Didn't you say you wanted to have a look at garden sheds?"

Mark's face lit up. He'd been poring over brochures and leaflets for weeks, weighing up the pros and cons of each design.

He seemed to be favouring a shed with an attached lean-to greenhouse. "So we can grow our own tomatoes," he'd enthused.

"Can't you grow tomatoes outside?" I'd asked.

"Yes. They often taste better, but they don't produce much fruit." I'd forgotten that the tomato for some strange reason was classified as a fruit.

"Shouldn't we wait until we know how much the boiler's going to cost before we start looking at sheds?" Mark went over to the boiler and flipped a couple of switches. The machine remained silent. "Damn thing." He gave it a slap.

"And did that make you feel better?" I smirked.

"Not really."

"About the shed," I said, peering out of the window again. "It won't cost anything to go look, and it beats staying here waiting for the place to warm up."

Mark shrugged, but I could tell he was excited at finally getting to go see actual sheds rather than just pictures of them.

"Didn't we get a leaflet through the letterbox a while ago advertising cut price sheds?" I asked, putting on my coat.

"Yeah, but the place was a good ten miles away."

"It pays to shop around, as Gran always tells me," I said, trying to imitate the old gal.

Mark laughed.

He lifted the car keys from their hook. "Want me to drive?"

I shrugged.

As I'd predicted, Mark had become a better and more confident driver than me. I didn't have a natural feel for the road, which was probably one of the reasons why after passing my test I hadn't immediately gone out and bought a car. That, and the cost of buying and maintaining a vehicle.

I turned off the oven and Mark put a guard around the fire.

"I'll just go and ask Paul if he knows a reliable heating engineer," I said when we were walking up the garden path.

"Don't you have a maintenance contract with someone?"

"No, I should get one organised though."

Mark said he'd stay in the car to start the engine and warm it up.

"Simon," Sam said, opening his front door.

"Hi, Sam, is your dad in? I want to ask him if he knows any good heating engineers—our boiler's stopped working."

"Ouch! Hang on, I'll go ask him," Sam said, leaving me stood outside in the rain.

"Oi, don't you invite visitors inside?" I shouted after him.

A sheepish Sam came back and ushered me inside. "Sorry."

After exchanging pleasantries with both Paul and Helen, Paul said he'd ring a mate of his.

"Do you know if he'll be able to come out tomorrow, because I'll have to arrange time off." I told him.

"That's all right," Helen put in. "I'm working here at home for the next few days. I'll let him in with Sam's key."

"Thanks, you've saved my life, both of you."

"I'll ask Don if he can fit you in tomorrow," Paul said,

picking up the phone. "You've no heat at all?"

"There's the coal fire of course, the cooker in the kitchen is still working, and I can heat up the water using the electric immersion heater. So we aren't desperate."

"There's no reply," Paul said, replacing the receiver. "Leave it with me. I'll call him again later."

"Thanks," I said. "I can't stop, Mark's in the car—we're about to go shed shopping."

Paul chuckled.

"Can I come?" Sam asked.

"That's 'May I come, please,'" Helen corrected. "And don't you think they see enough of you and Billy as it is?"

"Aw, Mum. They don't mind, do you?" Sam treated me to his most beguiling smile.

"What can I say?" I shrugged my shoulders at Paul and Helen.

"May I, Mum, please?"

"All right, but your dinner will be on the table at five o'clock. Don't be late."

"We'll have him back long before then," I said.

"I'll get my coat." Sam scampered off.

"If he gets too much, just tell us," Helen said.

I smiled and nodded. However, I seriously doubted we'd ever get to that stage.

A few moments later I heard feet pounding down the stairs. Sam popped his head around the living room door. "Come on, Simon, Mark's waiting."

"I've got my orders," I said, bidding Paul and Helen goodbye. They laughed.

ALL THE SHEDS were set up outside, not unsurprisingly, but it would have been nice to be able to look at them while staying dry. Fortunately the three of us were wearing waterproofs.

"That one's nice," Sam said, pointing to a huge marquee-sized building in dark wood that would probably qualify for its own postcode.

"Yeah, right," Mark said. "It's big enough to host a garden party inside it,"

"I think it's bigger than our yard," I said. Then I got a look at the price and turned away, feeling faint.

"I just said it was nice, that's all." Sam shrugged.

"How come we got lumbered with the kid anyway?" Mark asked me.

It must have been loud enough for Sam to hear because he said, "Because I'm irresistible."

"More like irrepressible," I said, watching him wander up and down.

"Or irri-pestible," Mark said.

"That's not a word." Sam looked over his shoulder at us and laughed.

Mark shook his head and we continued to look around.

"What about that one?" Mark pointed to a shed in a far corner.

"That's more like it," I said, once I'd seen the price. Though as soon as I got inside the shed I bumped my head.

"I think we ought to choose one where the roof is highest in the middle." The one I'd just gone inside had a sloping roof.

"They call them apex roofs," Sam said.

"Hark at the expert," Mark said, pinching one of Sam's cheeks.

"Geroff." Sam stepped back and onto my foot.

"I thought you wanted one with a greenhouse bit on it?" I questioned, shaking my foot.

"Have you seen the prices of those?" Mark pointed.

"Apart from tomatoes, what else could you use a greenhouse add-on thingy for?" I asked.

"I could bring on bedding plants."

I wasn't sure what he was going on about, but I didn't want to show my ignorance.

"And there's always the chance I might start to grow fruit."

"Wouldn't you need a heater for that?" Sam asked.

"Yeah, you've got a point there." Mark conceded. "I could also grow flowers." He lowered his voice. "Because I'd love to give you flowers I'd grown myself."

"Aw, sweet," Sam said. Evidently the kid had excellent hearing.

"If you need a greenhouse, then we'll have a greenhouse," I told Mark, brooking no argument.

His expression told me I'd be getting lucky later. I couldn't wait to get home.

The garden centre didn't have that many models to choose from, so Mark suggested a visit to the shed place we'd gotten the leaflet from. I agreed, but realised I'd have to wait for my reward.

It took some time to get to the "shed shop," as Sam called it.

"At least the rain's stopped," Sam said when we had finally arrived and were picking our way around the puddles in the pot-holed car park. "Wow, this is what I call a lot of sheds." He turned a corner and disappeared from view.

Everywhere we looked were sheds. Large, small, and many in between. There were wooden sheds, metal sheds, and some I wasn't sure what they were made of...plastic or fibreglass maybe.

We spent about an hour looking round. By the time Mark had made his decision—ten foot shed with an apex roof and an attached lean-to greenhouse—I was in serious need of a toilet so flagged down a passing sales assistant. I hadn't meant to buy the shed there and then, but by the time I'd come back from using the toilet the assistant was in full sales mode, and I realised I couldn't deny Mark any longer. Also, I hoped it would increase the value of my reward once we got home.

So we paid the deposit. The rest would be given to the erection crew after they built the shed.

We set off for home, me trying to sit still, knowing what awaited me when we got there.

"Can we stop at the pub?" Sam asked from the backseat.

No, I thought.

"You're turning into a boozer. Maybe we should get you home so you won't miss your dinner."

Yes!

"That's not for hours, and I'm not going to get drunk on half a shandy," Sam said.

"Simon?" Mark asked.

Shit! I sighed, knowing I couldn't deny Sam anything. My arse and Mark's dick would still be there later. "Okay, just a quick one. But just the one...Mark and I have to get the dinner on." I felt proud of myself for my quick thinking. If things went the way I hoped, we wouldn't be getting around to food until well into the evening.

"I'LL TRY TO light the boiler again," Mark said once we were back home.

"Sod the boiler," I said, pulling Mark towards me by his scarf. "You promised to light my boiler."

Mark smiled one of his devilish smiles. "Okay, you go up-stairs and I'll bring my matches."

We certainly needed some form of heat as we raced up-stairs; the bedroom was freezing. Still, it gave us another ex-cuse—not that we needed one—to undress quickly and dive under the covers.

"You're cold," Mark said.

You think? I thought.

"I think I should take your temperature."

"Huh?" I wasn't ill, was I?

"And I've got just the right tool to do it." He rubbed his hard dick against my leg.

"Oh," I said, the penny finally dropping.

I must have sounded stupid. But when Mark started to kiss me, I forgot all about being stupid; heck, if he carried on doing what he was doing, I'd soon forget my name. "Mark! Need you." Evidently I'd never forget his name.

"Patience, my love. You've been champing at the bit all afternoon."

"Who can blame me. Come on, fuck me." Normally I was one of the most meek and mild-mannered men you could hope to meet, but when Mark revved my engine as he was doing now, I became shameless in the language I used. And to prove it, I added, "Now, stud. Stick it in and ride me!"

Mark grinned. "Sure you don't want warming up more first?"

"I'm hot already." He had made me hot, and bothered, and…

Mark rolled over and went exploring in the bedside drawer on his side.

"Hurry."

Usually Mark made love to me in the missionary position, as he said he liked to look at me, God knows why. But I knew that would let in too much cold air under the covers, so I turned onto my stomach and spread my legs.

"Need to get some more condoms soon," Mark said, rolling back to me.

I hated buying them. I always thought the cashier at the chemist's was looking down on me, especially when I bought lube at the same time. I then hit on the idea of buying lube at one shop and condoms at another. Maybe I'd try to find a mail order company.

Mark's fingers found my waiting hole. I spread my legs even wider to give him better access.

First one, then two, and finally three fingers were inserted into me, Mark stopping every now and again to add more lube.

I was a lot looser back there than when we first started making love. But even after ten months Mark was solicitous of my comfort. I loved him for this, as well as many other things, but…"Get the fuck on with it!" I groused.

"Shouldn't that be 'get on with the fuck?'" he laughed.

"That's all I need, a bloody comedian."

"Ready now, Tiger?"

Sometimes Mark called me Tiger when he made love to me, because he said I became like a wild tiger in bed. I know he was being silly, but this was one of those 'other things' I loved him for.

Finally, after too long a wait, Mark settled his weight on top of me and began to slide his beautiful dick home where it belonged.

Even through my lust-crazed brain I had the sense to ask Mark if he'd put on a condom. I hadn't felt it, but then I'd had other things on my mind.

Mark kissed the back of my neck. "Of course. Will never put you in danger."

Okay, so I was close to bursting out crying, but as my face was pressed into the pillow, even if the odd tear did leak out, no one would know.

"Ready?" Mark asked.

Despite my hurry of earlier, now I had Mark's big dick up my arse, I was content just to stay as we were; Mark's body made for a wonderful heated blanket.

"Simon?"

"Hold me."

Mark wound his arms around me and started to kiss the back of my neck and shoulders. I hated it when I got all needy and vulnerable like this, but Mark was always great about it. In fact he told me more than once that he liked being my white knight or superhero. One day I'd have to buy him a Superman costume or something. He would look awesome in it, and the sex…"Oh, God."

"You okay?"

"Never better." It was true. I'd managed to lock away Pathetic Simon, and Sexually Aggressive Simon was taking control again. "Come on, fuck me with that huge dick of yours."

Mark obliged, and slowly began to pump his huge tool in and out. "Maybe there's something about the smell of creosote that gets you going," he panted.

"It's the smell of you," I moaned. "Come on, fuck me."

And Mark did. Within moments the headboard began to bump against the wall as Mark rocked in and out of me.

I lifted up to get a hand to my dick to bring myself off. This was the downside of making love in this position. Because of Mark's extra weight on top of me it wasn't easy to find room to comfortably stroke myself off.

"Let me," Mark grunted. "Lift up onto all fours."

I did, and Mark, magnificent swordsman that he was, didn't miss a stroke. The new position let in a draft under the blanket, but we'd generated enough heat of our own to not have it bother us.

Mark reached under me and took me in hand. It only took a few hard tugs and I squirted all over the bottom sheet, crying out as my spunk and energy left me almost simultaneously.

I flopped down to the mattress, Mark still inside me. However, I had enough strength and state of mind to squeeze down my anal muscles to bring Mark as much pleasure as I could.

Mark grunted his approval and switched into top gear to hasten his climax.

"Oh, God!" Mark bit into my shoulder.

His body went rigid, then began to twitch.

"Oh, God," he repeated, though much more softly.

"I'm warm now," I confessed, feeling safe, sleepy and satisfied.

"Me, too." Mark kissed the spot on my shoulder that he'd recently bitten. Then he rolled off me, but thankfully he didn't go far.

I was in the wet spot but, once Mark wrapped his protective arms around me, I didn't care.

Chapter 9

AT WORK THE next morning, I was surprised to find a postal order from Mrs Thompson paying for the book she'd damaged. I hadn't gotten around to informing the Council of her debt, so there wouldn't be any delay in Mrs T's house-moving plans. Not from my end anyway.

Once all the usual Monday morning tasks had been accomplished, I thought I'd earned a coffee break. I walked along the corridor and pushed open the door to the little kitchenette we'd had to battle so hard with the Council to obtain.

I found a very distraught Sally Timpson trying to stem a flood of tears.

Dabbing at her eyes, she sniffed and said, "I'm sorry."

I smiled. "Sometimes we need a good cry. If you want to

talk about it, you know where my office is."

She gave me a wan smile, nodded, and got up to leave. "Thanks. I'll just go and wash my face in the ladies, and I'll be all right again."

"Okay, but remember, if you want to talk about it…"

MY AFTERNOON MEETING at the Town Hall was as dull as ever. At least they served real coffee; it was about the only thing that kept me awake. The heating was on full blast, but apart from opening a window, the level of heat couldn't be regulated. The heating system in this example of municipal Victorian splendour was very inefficient. While we roasted, other rooms were cold and the workers there had to plug in electric fires.

The meeting finally ground to a close; I don't think I uttered a single word during the whole thing. It was only 3 P.M.; it wasn't worth going back to the library only to have to come back this way for the solicitors. I'd made a 4 P.M. appointment to see Mr Anderson about Fred's will. So, although I felt a bit uncomfortable about shopping during work time, I picked up a few items. It was an area of town I rarely visited.

Mark loved cheese. There was a reasonable selection at the supermarket, but as I passed it, I remembered how good the cheese was from the delicatessen on Mill Lane. The lane was hidden behind a number of large shops. I was amazed that the deli was able to survive in such an out of the way spot, but the products it sold were wonderful, if a little pricey, so I assumed its reputation for excellence kept it afloat.

The Deli reminded me of Gran's descriptions of shops she used to frequent in her youth. The floor was covered with brick-red tiles; the walls were of plain whitewash. A large number of foliage plants were placed all round the shop. They even had a wooden straight-backed chair next to the counter.

There was a wide variety of cheese to choose from. The

shopkeeper suggested I try a few of them on some small crackers he'd brought out. I knew I'd have to give Mark directions to this place; it would be his idea of heaven on earth. I spent a fortune, and no wonder the man asked me to "come again soon."

Although I'd be a few minutes early, I decided to head over to the solicitor's. I hoped the cheeses wouldn't start to release their pungent odours during the meeting. After pushing open the impressive glass-and-chrome door, I presented myself at the reception desk.

The same adenoidally-challenged woman who'd booked my appointment over the phone showed me into Mr Anderson's office. The solicitor asked if I wanted a cup of coffee, but I'd had more than my fill at the Town Hall.

"So, to business, Mr Peters," the solicitor said, leaning forward in his high-backed leather chair.

"I was surprised Mr Jones had left a will," I said, taking him at his word.

"Indeed," Mr Anderson said. "Mr Jones' estate wasn't a large one, but he had chosen to make a financial bequest to your library."

I raised an eyebrow. I had no idea Fred had any money.

Mr Anderson got out a sheaf of papers, glanced at them briefly, and said, "Mr Jones wanted to donate five hundred pounds to the reading room. However, he stipulated the sum must be spent on new furniture. He wishes the library to invest in a set of padded chairs."

I couldn't help my laugh. Fred would often complain about how hard the wooden seats were.

Mr Anderson's lips thinned. "Although it wasn't made a provision of the bequest, Mr Jones asked that a box containing his ashes be put in the reading room."

Both my eyebrows went up this time. "Oh…I, I've no idea if that would be allowed."

I could visualise the Council spending weeks—if not months—debating the issue. My right hand began to involuntarily ache at the prospect of having to fill in endless forms, in triplicate of course. And the publicity. Although newspaper coverage might be beneficial in highlighting the plight of the town's library with its slashed budgets, decreased opening hours, and...

Mr Anderson cleared his throat. "The box that contains Mr Jones's remains is nondescript. He seemed to think a plain wooden box," he paused to consult his papers, then quoted, "would 'best fit a plain and ordinary bloke like me.' It was Mr Jones's hope that such a receptacle wouldn't draw too much attention to itself if it were placed in the library."

I needed a moment to think. The money would certainly come in useful; the chairs in the reading room were old and scarred. But was I allowed to make such a decision?

Swallowing, and wishing I'd accepted the earlier offer of coffee, I asked, "This conversation, it is confidential?"

"Most certainly."

I took a deep breath and let it out. "It's unlikely anyone would, but what if you were asked what happened to Fred's remains?"

Mr Anderson smiled. "That would be covered by client confidentiality."

I sighed. "All right. I'll agree to the terms of Mr Jones's will." I supposed if we put Fred's ashes on a high shelf, no one would see them and start asking awkward questions.

"I can understand this is something of an unusual request," Mr Anderson conceded.

"Yes, it would put the readers off if they knew." I smiled.

"Quite so." He nodded. "Would you care to collect the box today? I would imagine the funeral director's will still be open." He made to pick up the telephone receiver on his desk.

"No," I said raising my voice. I didn't much fancy carrying around a box of ashes. I certainly didn't want to put them in the same bag as Mark's cheeses. "Would it be all right if I collected them later in the week?"

"I'm sure that will be fine. I will arrange for the cheque to be posted to you shortly."

I thanked him. "This business with Fred has made me think about my own situation."

Mr Anderson nodded in understanding.

"I'd like to make an appointment with you so I can draw up a will."

Checking his wristwatch he said, "I don't have any more appointments today, so we can get the ball rolling now if you like?"

I hadn't expected this, but I gave my agreement.

Mr Anderson reached for a legal pad. "Many people your age neglect this most important matter."

"Yes, I can see why, but there's a reason why I need everything to be in order should I die unexpectedly."

Mr Anderson gave a slight nod.

I didn't relish the prospect of outing myself, but there was no choice, so I told him about my relationship with Mark, and how he wouldn't have any legal right to my estate should anything happen to me.

"I completely understand, Mr Peters. I drew up the same documents for my partner Dennis and myself." He pointed to a framed picture on his desk of a younger man, who looked quite handsome in a boy-next-door sort of way.

"Oh, right." I couldn't think of anything more sensible to say.

Fortunately, Mr Anderson did. "If you want to do things properly, you ought to set up powers of attorney..." He went on to detail a whole load of other documents which would give Mark as many rights as possible should I fall ill, be incapacitated, or worse. And of course I'd get the same benefits if, God forbid, anything should happen to Mark.

"As gay men," Mr Anderson continued, "we have very few automatic rights, so we have to jump through an alarming number of hoops in order to get something close to what a heterosexual married couple receive without question."

I nodded.

"I could tell you any number of horror stories where one

partner in a gay relationship dies and the other is totally frozen out by the deceased partner's family. One or two were even prevented from attending their lover's funeral."

"That's horrible," I said. "I want to make Mark's and my relationship as legally watertight as possible."

We talked for a few more minutes, and I agreed to bring Mark along at the same time a week later. Mark would have finished work, and I could wangle getting out an hour early.

"HI, LUUUCY, I'M hooome!" I called out as usual.

I'd stopped doing this a while ago, thinking it was getting a bit old, and I wasn't sure if Mark really appreciated me saying it anyway. However, after a few days of just coming through the door, Mark questioned me about the change. When I explained my reasoning, he told me not to be so daft, that he loved hearing it.

"Hi," Mark said, poking his head round the kitchen door.

I put the bag of cheeses on the floor and held out a dozen red roses. I'd picked them up at the florists opposite the solicitor's.

He looked surprised, but this was soon replaced by a wide smile.

"They're wonderful," he said, taking the bouquet from me and bringing his face close to the blooms.

Alas, they didn't have much of an aroma. The lady in the shop had told me in order to grow longer-lasting and prettier roses, the scent was often lost in the hybriding process.

After thanking me with several kisses, Mark took the flowers into the kitchen. Once he'd arranged them in a vase, he turned round and took me into his arms.

We spent a good few minutes just holding, kissing, and caressing one another.

"Oh, I almost forgot."

I disengaged from Mark's embrace and went back into the front room. Coming back I opened the shopping bag on the counter and showed him the cheeses.

"We'll have some after dinner on those crackers we got last week."

I nodded, sharing in Mark's delight as he read the labels that the shopkeeper had stuck on each small parcel.

It was only at this point that I realised the boiler was working again.

"Helen said that Paul's' mate came round to fix it this morning." Mark reached over and showed me the bill.

"Crikey, we're in the wrong jobs," I told him glancing at the final total.

"I know, but at least we're nice and warm again."

"True, but it was kind of nice snuggling up to you last night," I said, waggling my eyebrows.

He laughed before continuing his meal preparations. From the looks of things, we were having beef stew and dumplings. This was one of my favourite winter meals.

During dinner I brought up the potentially sensitive subject of our mortality.

"It's something I don't want to think about," Mark admitted. "But I know we have to."

"I agree. I just want to get the papers signed, put them away and hope we won't need to use them for a long time."

Mark nodded.

"One last thing, then we can forget about it till next week. If I die while I'm still working for the Council my next of kin would get a lump sum. Mum has always been listed as that, but tomorrow I'm going to fill out the forms changing it to you."

Mark reached over the table and squeezed my hand. "If you died, no amount of money could replace you."

I returned his squeeze.

THE RAIN WAS pelting down heavily, our umbrellas doing little to stop us from getting soaked as we stood at the graveside.

Try as hard as I might, my gaze kept snapping back to the brass plate affixed to the oak coffin bearing the simple but stark statement:

Mark James Smith 1966-1987

…though it was often difficult to make out the words as the rain spattered the plate, to say nothing of the tears filling my eyes.

Through my tears I took in the huddle of black-garbed figures around me. I saw Mary and Jerry, my mum and dad, Tom, Cliff, and Tim. Paul and Helen were supporting Sam. Daphne was standing next to them, clutching a sodden handkerchief. All were gazing down into the open dark maw of the grave.

The vicar, his sodden clerical clothing billowing in the angry wind, held an umbrella in one hand and a prayer book in the other. The familiar words of the committal service drifted over the sorry scene.

Then Roy, Mark's father, a man who stood over six feet tall, his wet, black hair plastered to his scalp, limped up to the coffin. He leant on his walking stick and put his remaining hand onto his son's casket immediately prior to it being lowered. "I'm so sorry. I wish I'd had gotten to know you—I always loved you."

My gaze fixed itself yet again to the brass plate; I watched transfixed as it and the box containing my lover were slowly lowered into the darkness.

"Noooooooooo!" I cried out, fighting to get to the coffin. My arms and legs wouldn't work properly, and I felt like I was swimming through dark treacle. Disembodied sounds and images filled my head; it was as though I were being sucked into a deep, dark abyss.

"Simon, Simon, wake up!"

The scene changed—I was sitting bolt upright in bed. I wasn't standing in the graveyard, and Mark, my awesome, beautiful Mark, was holding me.

I was shaking and couldn't seem to stop. Throwing my arms around Mark, I said, "Thank God. You're here, you're alive."

"Yes, I'm here."

"I…I dreamed I was at your funeral. It was horrible."

"It was a nightmare…not real. I'm here, I don't plan on going anywhere, not for another fifty or sixty years, anyway." He gently rocked me in his arms and stroked my back.

I still had a terrible fear that my dream might be some kind of premonition. I remembered the dates on the coffin. There were still a couple of months left to run this year.

I remembered seeing Roy. "What does your dad look like?"

"Huh?"

If his description fitted the person I'd seen, then what I'd dreamt could still come true. I knew as soon as I'd asked the question I was being stupid.

"Dad's a bit shorter than me, about five feet seven or so. He has sandy-blonde hair that's going white at the temples. His eyes are a sort of bluish green." Mark kissed my cheek. "Might be a strange question to ask, but why did you want to know? Was Dad in your nightmare?"

I nodded as relief flooded through me. "He put his hand on your coffin and said that he loved you, and he was sorry for all the things he'd done to you."

"Oh."

"But he didn't look anything like what you've just described, so it's okay. But I bet some part of the real Roy is sorry." I don't know why I added that last, but I felt it as though it were fact.

"I doubt it." Mark scoffed.

"Sorry, love," It was now my turn to comfort Mark. "It's his loss. He can't see what I'm seeing. You're amazing, kind, special, loving, gentle…"

Mark kissed my lips to shut me up.

"Everything I said was true."

Mark shook his head. "All this comes from us talking about death and dying last night, and you would insist on having some more of that cheese for supper. Didn't I say it would give you bad dreams?"

I nodded, feeling even more foolish for waking Mark up as he had to get up early for work.

Fortunately the nightmare didn't recur; however, neither of us knew then that very soon we would all be plunged into a real-life nightmare.

Chapter 10

THERE WAS A brief tap at my office door before Sally poked her head round it.

"Got a minute?"

"Sure, come in." I gestured to one of my guest chairs.

I'd read that for a personal conversation—I was assuming Sally was seeing me on a personal matter—it was best not to have a desk separating us. So I got up, walked round my desk, and took the other chair.

"How are you today?"

Sally shook her head. "I've been better."

I put on a sympathetic face and gave her the space to talk.

"Would it be all right if I had a few days off?"

"I can't see why not. Sandra should be able to cope, and I

can always lend a hand if necessary."

She nodded.

"Hang on, I'll get the leave book." I stood and retrieved the ledger from my desk drawer. Leafing through it I found Sally's page. "You have five days still owing to you."

"Yes I know, and they'll have to last me until April, too."

"If it's a family emergency, I can arrange compassionate leave." That would give her up to three days, and it wouldn't eat into her regular leave entitlement.

She paused before asking, "Can you treat this conversation as confidential?"

I hesitated.

"It's nothing criminal," she assured me. "Stupid, but not criminal."

I nodded. "Okay, then whatever you say won't leave this room."

"Thanks. I've been seeing my boyfriend, George, for a couple of years now. We met at university."

I'd seen George at a few Council social functions; he was pretty hot, if you went for the muscular sporty look.

"A couple of weeks ago I discovered my period was late. I did a home test and it came up positive."

"I see." I didn't think she'd want me to congratulate her, given her previous words.

"George didn't take the news well. He wanted," she swallowed, "he wanted…" She sniffed and began to blink rapidly.

I wasn't much use at comforting females, and of course there was little I could say regarding her pregnancy. Like any decent boss, I had a box of Kleenex on my desk. I pushed a couple into her palm and squeezed her shoulder. I made a few what I hoped were comforting noises and waited till she'd calmed down.

"Thanks," she said once she'd gotten control of her emotions. "George wants me to have an abortion."

"And you don't."

"I'm Catholic."

That didn't really give me an answer, but I was tactful enough not to point that out.

"So I need the time off to think and to tell my family about it all."

"And George, will he support you?"

She laughed. "That stupid prick just wants to bury his head in the sand in the hope that it'll all go away. Well, it won't."

"No." I paused. "Of course you can take three days compassionate leave, and no one will learn from me the reason."

"DO YOU MIND if I stop a bit later tonight?" Mark asked as we did the washing up that evening.

"Of course not."

Mark had started taking evening classes on catering management at the local college.

"The other guys on the course usually go down the Kings Head for a pint afterwards. They've asked me a few times if I wanted to join them, but I've always said no."

"Why didn't you go with them before?"

"I like spending my evenings with you."

"And now you've grown tired of me." I pretended to look upset.

"Daft bugger." He flicked some dish water at me. "I'll be back by ten at the latest."

I'D GOTTEN LOST in a book, something I usually did on Mark's college nights. Feeling a need to stretch, I glanced over at the mantle clock. It was a quarter past ten. I wasn't worried…much.

I tried to get back into my book, but it was no good. Standing, I walked over to the window and peeked through the curtains at an empty street. We didn't get much through traffic, so when I heard a car coming, and it seemed to slow down, I began to relax. However, the car passed the window; it wasn't ours.

I put on my coat and took a stroll down the street. There was nothing to see, so I came back home, hoping the phone hadn't rung in my absence.

I looked at the clock again; half ten. I couldn't seem to settle down to do anything, so I went into the kitchen to make a drink.

I sat at the kitchen table and sipped at my cocoa, trying to quell my rising anxiety. I knew Mark had to get up early for work the next day, so he wouldn't stay out late…

Unless something's happened to him, a mental voice announced.

I didn't like where that thought took me, so I tried to change track. I turned the radio on and tuned it to some relaxing music. Retaking my seat, I finished my drink.

Could that stupid nightmare be coming true, was Mark lying injured somewhere? My thoughts were interrupted by the noise of a key turning in the lock. I got to my feet, relief washing over me.

Mark came into the kitchen—all smiles. "I saw Daphne in the pub, and she said that as I was doing this course for work, she'd let me start later on Wednesday mornings."

"Couldn't you have rung and told me?" Relief was turning to anger.

"Sorry." Mark's smile fell. "I forgot all about the time."

I couldn't stay mad at him. Those puppy-dog eyes did it for me every time. I gave him a hug. He smelt of cigarette smoke.

"Come up to bed." I kissed his cheek.

"Probably should have a bath first."

"Okay, but don't be long. I want you to show me just how sorry you really are." I gave his tight bum cheeks a squeeze.

He laughed and chased me up the stairs.

After his bath, Mark came into the bedroom, a towel wrapped around his waist. Seeing me lying naked on the bed, he loosened the knot on the towel. The terry cloth fell to the floor, revealing Mark in all his stunning glory. He licked his lips and began to stroke his erecting dick.

"You've been a naughty boy," I said, beckoning him with a finger.

"I'm sorry, sir."

Occasionally Mark and I played sexual games, although this was the first time dominance and submission had been a part of them. That lifestyle hadn't interested me, but I was willing to try anything once.

"Come here and take your punishment like a man."

"You will be gentle with me, won't you?"

"I might be persuaded to be lenient. But it will take a lot of persuading."

Mark licked his lips again.

I patted the bed. "On your back."

He complied and I ran my fingertips lightly over his wide chest. Starting again at his feet, my fingertips swept up his legs, avoiding his groin. I moved up to his belly, circled round his navel and glided up to his face, a face that still stunned me with its beauty.

Leaning forward, I licked at Mark's sensitive nipples, scraping the left one with my front teeth. Mark's left nipple, I'd discovered, was far more sensitive than his right. It was something I often took full advantage of. I blew softly over the now moistened nub.

Mark began to move his hands toward his dick; I batted them away. This would be his punishment. I wouldn't touch him down there, and he wasn't allowed to, either.

He pouted, a wonderful look on him, so much so I had to interrupt my ministrations to his chest and kiss those full, moist lips. So lost was I in exploring his mouth I almost forgot about my stated aim to tease Mark into a state of sexual arousal.

Eventually, I moved on to Mark's right ear, which I licked, sucked, and lightly bit. This, I knew, would drive him mad. He again tried to touch himself, and again I stopped him.

"Do that again and I'll tie your hands."

He smirked. I took that as a challenge, and although we weren't into bondage, I decided to accept it as such.

Moving on to licking behind his ear, another erogenous zone for him, I saw Mark reach for his now fully erect and leaking dick.

Wordlessly I got off the bed and went to the wardrobe, coming back with a handful of my ties.

"You asked for it."

Mark got one of the most evil, smug, and satisfied smiles on his face that I'd ever seen. It had been a trap, and I'd fallen right into it.

Making short work of securing his hands—I never knew I was that good at knots, never having been in the boy scouts—I continued with my "punishment."

Sweeping my tongue slowly down the side of his face, I paused briefly to chew on his neck.

I moved downward, bypassing his straining dick, and began to suck on his balls, another sensitive area, one that always got Mark's motor running.

"Simon!" he gasped.

After spending about five minutes attending to Mark's balls and their furry sac, I moved downward to his taint—a word I'd never even heard of before Mark—and licked my way slowly downward to his arse crack. Mark raised his legs to allow me easier access, but with his hands tied to the headboard I knew he wouldn't be able to keep them raised for long. Sure enough, they soon rested on my back.

Making my tongue into a point, I poked at Mark's opening. He gasped but I was soon allowed entry. I was glad he'd recently bathed—all I could smell and taste was clean Mark, one of the best taste-smell combinations ever created.

"God!" Mark panted as I sucked on his arse lips, making a meal of it.

I pulled back and blew a steady stream of warm air onto

Mark's spit-slicked ring. It had the desired effect, Mark jolted upward, and I had to grab his legs to keep him in place.

Although Mark usually topped because I preferred it that way, my own hard erection was demanding attention, and what better attention could I give it than allowing it to bury itself in Mark's inviting warmth?

Crawling backward I got off the bed and, on hands and knees, made my way over to the bedside table for supplies.

"Hurry," Mark gasped.

Just to tease him further—he was being punished, after all—I deliberately took my time finding a condom and the tube of lube.

"Get the fuck on with it."

"Don't you mean 'get on with the fuck?'" I grinned.

"Simon!"

I held up the foil packet. "Want to put this on for me? Oh," I smiled, trying to make it look sincere, "I forgot, you can't."

"Bastard," I could see the muscles in his arms flexing, but he wasn't going anywhere. I hoped I'd still be able to wear those ties afterward, but if not, it was a sacrifice worth making.

Slowly, with infinite care, I ripped open the packet and extracted the disc.

I remembered then that Mark could probably apply the condom with his mouth, but that would give him too much pleasure. So I decided to roll it on myself, taking my own sweet time about it, of course.

Then came the lubing-up. Mark had told me often enough that there was no such thing as too much lube. The squishing, sucking noise it made as I slowly wanked myself was turning me on. A quick glance over at Mark told me it was having the same effect on him.

When I climbed back onto the bed Mark lifted his legs and I quickly found and began to circle his opening with a finger. He'd closed up during the last few minutes, so I had to work at it to gain entrance. I could tell Mark was straining to open up, but as this wasn't his usual role when we made love, he was out of practice.

My finger went in to the first knuckle before his anal muscles grabbed hold of my finger.

I soon was able to get the entire finger in, moving—more slowly than was strictly necessary—followed by a second digit. Mark was whimpering, but I knew it was due to a combination of anticipation, impatience, frustration, and need, and not pain.

I separated my two fingers, which soon allowed for the addition of a third. Twisting them around, I got Mark used to the sensation.

"Ready?" I asked.

"Been fucking ready for ages," Mark groaned.

I knew that wasn't true. If I'd have entered him sooner it would've hurt, and I never wanted to do that. He'd intimated that some of his clients hadn't been gentle and...I shook my head, determined not to think about that now. Instead I concentrated on guiding myself inside of Mark. He was so warm, tight, and just plain amazing.

Mark began to milk my dick and I had to fight the urge not to come there and then.

"Two can play this game," Mark said, smiling up at me.

I slapped his hip, pretty hard.

"Ouch! What did you do that for?" Mark wanted to know.

"Because I can," I grinned at him.

Feeling I could move without fear of losing my load, I slowly eased out. Mark whimpered, but soon shut up when I slid home again.

My strokes grew more rapid. No way was I going to last long; Mark was pulling out all the stops to send me over the edge as quickly as he could. In addition to the cock-milking, he blew kisses at me that were punctuated by moans and the most dirty of porn talk. To hear him, I was the next best thing to Jeff Stryker, something I knew was definitely not the case, but it was nice to hear anyway.

"You bastard," I ground out through clenched teeth as I felt my orgasm approach. No way could I stop it. I didn't want to. I yelled, every muscle in my body going tight as I shot God knew how many times into the condom.

Panting and sweating, I fell exhaustedly on top of Mark. He too was bathed in sweat. Through the post-coital haze I could feel Mark's huge erection pressing into my groin. He hadn't gotten off, or more accurately I hadn't helped him to get off. I started to feel guilty, but soon changed my mind.

Pulling out, I rolled off my lover and stared up at the ceiling. "Oh," I panted, my heart still beating rapidly. "Thank you; that was one of the best orgasms I've had in a long time."

"What about me?" Mark asked softly.

"Think I might take a bath, I could do with one."

"Simon."

"Yeah, a nice long soak after draining my balls, can't think of a better way to end the day."

"Simon!" Mark growled.

"Sorry, you said something?" I propped my head up on a bent arm and looked over at my frustrated lover.

"Either untie me or get me off."

"Oh, I don't know, I kind of like you tied up like this and at my mercy." My dick, which had begun to soften, stiffened up at the thought of being able to tease Mark some more. But the condom was cold, wet, and slimy.

Feeling devilish, I pulled the rubber off and smeared its contents over Mark's smooth, flat belly. Then I began to draw patterns in the goo. I knew Mark was ticklish there, and sure enough he began to thrash around. I moved to sit on his thighs to keep him in place.

"Simon, do something, now!"

I couldn't deny him any longer. So I slid down his legs until we were lying cock to mouth.

"Condom," Mark whimpered.

Normally having to use condoms didn't bother me, but

hell, they were sure getting in the way tonight.

Unlike last time, I didn't mess about rolling the rubber down Mark's weeping cock.

I didn't much care for the taste of latex, but there was no option if I wanted to lick my man. Starting at the base I slowly ran my tongue up to the tip. After swirling around the head a few times I licked my way down the other side.

"Suck on it, Goddamn it!"

So I did. And I amazed myself by being able to deep throat him on the third attempt. Mark screamed. I feared the neighbours would start banging on the wall, so I did my best to bring Mark off as quickly as I could using a combination of mouth and hands.

Within moments I felt Mark's balls draw up, and he whimpered and went rigid. The rubber ballooned up, I pulled off and gave him a few more strokes with my hand.

"Oh, God, oh, God." Mark muttered, but at least he was being quiet.

I pulled off his condom and added its contents to the cold mess on his chest.

"Simon, let me loose, my arms are starting to cramp and I need to pee."

"Sorry."

Mark had pulled the knots tight and they took some undoing, but finally I managed to set him free.

Rubbing at Mark's wrists, I mused aloud that our brief foray into bondage had been fun.

"For you."

"You didn't enjoy it? You got off...eventually." I grinned.

"True. But next time, you'll be the one who'll be getting tied up."

My tired dick twitched in anticipation.

❖

"YOU'RE LATE," MARY said as I signed in at work the next morning.

I felt my face heat.

"What?" Mary got that twinkle in her eye.

I knew I'd have to tell her something. Involuntarily I rubbed at my wrists.

When Mark had awoken he wanted to take advantage of the extra time Daphne had given him, so out came my ties again, with me on the receiving end, so to speak. We'd enjoyed ourselves so much, we'd lost track of the time.

"Let's just say I was tied up this morning."

I could almost see the cogs turning in her head. "You dirty buggers!"

"Shush." I took a look around, but fortunately no one was close by.

"I want details," she said, following me to my office.

"Sod off!"

I'd already said too much, and Mary's dirty mind had managed to fill in the rest. I wished I'd told her my alarm clock had broken and Mark and I had overslept. I knew now that Mary had sensed something juicy and she wouldn't let go of it.

"Don't be mean. I'll tell you all about Jerry and me." She smiled, knowing I wasn't interested, not in the female part of that equation anyway.

I walked along the corridor to my office and beckoned for Mary to follow. "Need a quick word."

"Okay." She entered the office after me and closed the door.

I sat behind my desk and gestured for Mary to take a seat. Then I told her about Fred's request to have his ashes placed in the reading room.

"Yuck! I hope he won't haunt the place."

"Come on, Fred was harmless enough when he was alive...he'll hardly start acting nasty now he's dead."

"Suppose, but why do we have to have his ashes? We're a library, not a...mausoleum."

I shook my head; I'd hoped I'd be able to get Mary onside with this. Conscious that she needed to get to her department, I quickly explained about the five hundred pounds, and what Fred wanted the money spent on.

She laughed.

I swore her to secrecy about Fred's remains; she promised not to even tell John, her work colleague and my successor.

JUST BEFORE I left the office on Thursday night, I got a call from a surprisingly happy Sally Timpson. She'd thought something was wrong "down below" and, on going to see her doctor, it had been confirmed that she had had a miscarriage.

"Oh, I…" Again, I wasn't sure if commiserations or congratulations were in order.

"It's good news, Simon," she said, saving me the trouble of having to choose. "I'll be back at work tomorrow."

After telling Sally that she'd been missed, we hung up and I finally left the library for the day.

Mark was waiting outside in the car. It was raining rather heavily. I thanked him for being so thoughtful, and he drove us to the supermarket, then to the take-away for our traditional Chinese meal. We'd eaten practically everything on their menu that had appealed to us, so we'd begun to cycle through the choices for the third, or was it the fourth, time?

In bed that night Mark asked, "So do you want to?"

I decided to play dumb. "To what?"

"Rumpy pumpy, a bit of how's your father, you know, play hide the sausage?"

Trying not to laugh at Mark's comic euphemisms, I said, "Sorry, dear, I've got a headache." I couldn't keep the act up any longer, and I burst out laughing.

"You sod!" He said, pinning me to the mattress. We enjoyed a leisurely lovemaking session, this time free of any bindings.

❖

IT WAS GREAT to wake up at my usual time, Mark still in bed with me. He'd booked the day off to be in for the shed delivery people.

"We have time, don't we?" Mark asked, his sleep-roughened voice instantly turning me on.

I glanced at the alarm clock. We didn't. And I couldn't be late two days running, it would set a bad example. But we did have time for some kissing and fondling.

The ringing of the telephone interrupted our make-out session. It was on my side of the bed, so I picked up the receiver. "Hello?" I said, trying to keep the frustration out of my voice.

"Thank God you're still there!"

"Cliff?" I sat more upright in the bed, my heart beginning to beat heavily at his distraught tone. "What's wrong?"

"The hospital. It's Tom. He, he's been stabbed!"

Chapter 11

I WASN'T SURE I'd heard Cliff correctly

"Did you say he'd been stabbed?"

Next to me, Mark gasped and clutched at my arm.

"Yes." Cliff sniffed. "The nurse, or whoever she was, said Tom was in the operating theatre."

"Oh, no. Why? Do you know what happened?"

Cliff started to cry. "A member of the public found him collapsed and bleeding. Tom was on his postal round."

"Oh, no," I repeated. I started to shiver. Mark pulled me closer and rubbed my arm. Trying to focus, I asked, "Do you want us to come over?"

"You've got work and—"

"That doesn't matter." I took the decision from him and

said Mark and I would be there within the hour.

"Thanks." Cliff sniffed. "I can't start the car, and I want to go see Tom and…"

"It's okay, we'll take you to the hospital."

There were more tears. "I didn't know who else to ask."

"Is there anyone who could stay with you until we get there?"

"No, I tried Al and Keith, but they're out of town. The only other person would be Tim, but…"

"I understand." Tim was a great guy, but he was a fusspot and would be more of a hindrance than a help in a crisis. "I want you to pack a bag for Tom. He'll need pyjamas, toiletries, and stuff like that."

"That's a good idea."

"And pack a few things for yourself, too. Just in case."

"Thanks, yes. I hadn't thought of that."

"We'll be with you soon. Hang in there. Tom's a fighter, he'll be okay." Of course I didn't know that for sure, but hopefully it would help.

We hung up and I turned into Mark's arms, seeking comfort and reassurance. As he held me I told him the parts of the conversation he hadn't heard.

"We'd better get dressed. Maybe we can grab breakfast at the hospital or something," I said, not feeling terribly hungry.

Mark kissed me and got out of bed. "I'll need to go see Helen before we go."

"Why?" Then I remembered. "The shed. It's okay if you'd rather stay here and—"

"Of course I'm coming with you. I'll just tell Helen where the men should build the shed."

"Thanks." I was glad I wouldn't have to face this crisis alone.

Once we'd gotten dressed, I rang Mary at home and told her why I wouldn't be at work.

When we knocked on the Bates's door, Paul answered. He looked like he was on his way to work.

I explained about Tom and that we had to leave for York.

Helen, who was spooning mashed-up food into Charlotte's mouth, sympathised, and before we could ask, volunteered to supervise the shed crew.

"Thanks," Mark said. "That's one less thing to worry about."

I handed Helen our receipt and a cheque to give to the crew once the thing was up.

Sam came into the kitchen. "Hi, guys." He looked at first Mark then me. "What's wrong?"

We knew Sam thought a great deal about Tom, and the older man had a strong bond with Sam. So I had to tread carefully as I told him what we knew, which was precious little.

Sam turned white. He opened his mouth, closed it again, swallowed, and asked, "Will he be all right?"

"We hope so," Mark said, resting a hand on the teen's shoulder. "All we know is that he's in the operating theatre now."

"Can I go with Simon and Mark?" Sam asked his father.

"Tom will be pretty ill, and you could get in the way. They might not even let you see him."

Sam tried to persuade his dad that he needed to go.

"What about school?" Helen asked, lifting Charlotte out of her high chair and rubbing her back.

"I wouldn't be able to concentrate on my schoolwork knowing Tom was..." Sam swallowed. "Hurt."

Paul looked over at us. "Would you rather go on your own?"

Sam turned his pleading eyes to us.

"Even if they let us see Tom, it won't be for long, and only in ones and twos. There'll be a lot of waiting around and you'll be bored," I told Sam.

"Please!" he entreated.

Mark and I communicated silently for a few seconds. I was conscious that we had to make a decision quickly, as we needed to get on the road. Mark gave a brief nod.

"Okay," I said, "but, as I said before, you might not even get to see Tom."

"I understand, but I'll be there for Cliff, too."

I was surprised and impressed at Sam's mature thinking.

"Take some of your homework," Helen told him. "Like Simon said, there'll be a lot of waiting around."

"Thanks, Mum." Sam raced out of the kitchen and up the stairs.

RUSH HOUR TRAFFIC was bad on the motorway. Mark was at the wheel and I sat worrying that we wouldn't be with Cliff within the hour like I'd promised.

In the end it took us about an hour and a quarter to get to Cliff and Tom's place.

Cliff must have been watching out for us, because he was coming down the garden path as we were getting out of the car.

Mark gave Cliff a silent hug.

"I feel numb. It hasn't sunk in yet. Not properly, anyway." Cliff said, turning to me. "Thanks for coming."

"Is there any more news?" I asked, giving Cliff my own hug.

"The last time I called they said he was still in theatre. I don't think they'll tell me much more than that over the phone."

I nodded.

We got into the car. Mark was driving again; Cliff sat in the front seat giving directions.

I asked Cliff if he'd rung Tom's parents. He had; they lived over in Cheshire and would be there in a couple of hours or so.

Another fifteen minutes saw us crawling round the hospital's car parks; there were very few available spots. I assumed the crush was due to people attending the various outpatient clinics. It was a bit too early for regular hospital visiting.

Sam spotted someone vacating a space and pointed it out to Mark, who drove just past it and reversed back into it. A guy in a black Volvo frowned his annoyance at missing the space.

Mark gave the man a little wave. "All's fair in love and car parking, mate," he said softly.

Through the mirror, I was pleased to see a slight smile on Cliff's lips.

❖

"CAN I HELP you?" asked the pleasant-looking woman behind the accident and emergency counter.

"Thomas Jenkinson. I got a call telling me he'd been attacked, and he'd been brought in here," Cliff told her.

The woman shuffled a couple of sheets of paper. "Are you a relative?"

I knew this was bound to be asked, and apparently, Cliff did, too.

"Yes, I'm his domestic partner."

To her credit, the woman didn't bat an eyelid. "Yes, Mr...?"

"Haldaine."

"Okay, Mr Haldaine, you need to take the lift or the stairs up to the next level, turn left and follow the signs to Bennett Ward, they should be able to give you more information there."

I could see how distraught Cliff was, so I thanked the lady and began shepherding him toward the lifts.

There were a number of people waiting for the lifts, so I decided it would be quicker to take the stairs. Besides, I had an irrational fear of lifts, always imagining myself being trapped in one.

As we walked along the corridors on the next level, I looked round at the shoddy décor. The walls were painted an unattractive institutional green. The paint was flaking away in places to reveal the creamy plaster underneath. My nose was assaulted by disinfectant and boiled cabbage. Thankfully, the latter seemed to fade as we walked along. Spotting the sign for Bennett Ward, Cliff paused outside the door.

"Now I'm actually here, I'm scared to go in."

I gave him a sympathetic smile.

Cliff pushed open the door and we all filed through. He knocked on a door marked *Sister's Office.*

"Enter!" a stern female voice said.

Mark and I stayed outside, but as Sam had stuck himself to Cliff's side, the two of them obeyed the command. The door remained partially open, so we were able to hear what was going on.

"Yes?" the same clipped voice asked.

"My name is Cliff Haldaine, my partner is Thomas Jenkinson. He was admitted to this ward earlier today."

"Are you a relative?"

"Yes, I just told you, he's my partner."

"Business partner?"

This didn't sound good.

"Domestic partner."

"It's hospital policy only to allow family members to see patients outside of visiting hours. Come back at two."

"He's my father," Sam piped up.

"Do you have any form of identification?" She sounded like she didn't believe Sam.

"I didn't think I'd need any."

"Good answer," I whispered to Mark, who grinned.

"But if your father is err...?"

"Look, Sister," Cliff put in. "We want to see Tom, not have a discussion about our family tree. Now which bed is he in, assuming he's not still in theatre?"

There was a pause, then the sister said, "Mr Jenkinson came back from recovery about fifteen minutes ago, but he's still drowsy. Like I said, visiting hours start at two."

"Are you saying I can't see my dad?" Sam persisted.

"Maybe for a few minutes. But I'm not sure you can see him." This last must have been addressed to Cliff.

"I want my uncle with me, you don't want me to start crying and creating a fuss in the ward if I get upset, do you?" Sam said, hopefully not overplaying his part.

"This is all very irregular," the sister huffed. "But if you promise to not disturb Mr Jenkinson, or any of my other patients, then you may sit with him for a few minutes, but only for a few minutes, mind."

"That's all we ask," Cliff said.

"Very well," We could hear the scraping of a chair, so Mark and I moved away from the door. The trio emerged, the battle-axe in blue leading the way.

"Yes?" she barked, fixing her icy glare on us. "Visiting time is not until two o'clock."

"We're with them," Mark said. No doubt to forestall another lengthy inquisition, he added, "but we'll stay in a waiting room or something."

"Very well." She nodded at Mark before sailing past. "Wait in there," she pointed to her right, never breaking step.

Mark and I entered the alcove she'd indicated. It had plastic chairs lining the walls, with a heavy-looking coffee table in the middle. A quick peek at the magazines laid out with military precision at one end of the table confirmed they were well out of date. "And I thought the ones at the library were old," I said, picking up an ancient edition of *Reader's Digest*.

I sat next to Mark, who whispered, "I met types like that sister last year when I was in the General. If we wait till she goes back into her lair, we can sneak a look at Tom. She'll become too busy with other things, and she won't bother checking."

I nodded. "The sister I spoke to on your ward seemed nice enough."

"She was—it was the other one who could give Joseph Goebbels a run for his money."

I smiled and tried to interest myself in an article about ancient Greek astrology.

A few moments later I heard footsteps. Looking up, I saw the sister walking past. She paid us no attention.

We waited a few more minutes, then Mark stuck his head around the corner. The coast must have been clear, because he gestured for me to follow him. We crept along the corridor, giving me the feeling we were trying to gain access to a top-secret military facility, not visit a friend.

Through a window, I saw Sam and Cliff sitting by a bed. They were in a single-occupancy side ward.

At least Tom will get some privacy having a room to himself, I thought.

Approaching, I could see Tom. He looked painfully white; I guessed this was due to the loss of blood. He had an IV drip going into his arm and another tube came from under a bandage on his chest. The only other piece of medical equipment seemed to be an oxygen mask.

"Hi," Mark said quietly.

Cliff was sitting in one of the bedside chairs, tightly holding on to his partner's hand.

Sam looked up. "The sister said he'll be all right. The knife missed all his vital organs."

I winced.

"He came round for a minute when we entered," Cliff whispered, "but he's sleeping again now."

"Best thing for him," I said, getting a little closer.

"Sam, do you want to come with us, and we'll let Cliff have a couple of minutes alone with Tom?" I suggested.

Sam nodded, and we made our way back to the plastic chairs.

"He looks so pale," Sam said, biting at his lip.

"Yeah." Mark reached over and patted Sam's hand. "You really helped earlier."

Sam turned and buried his face in Mark's shoulder.

TIME SEEMED TO drag. I continued reading my article, Mark had picked up a motor racing magazine, and Sam was half-heartedly doing his geography homework.

I heard the tip tap of shoes and knew the sister was coming. Looking up, I saw she had an older-looking couple with her.

"And here's your grandson," she said to the couple. "Where's the other…gentleman?"

"I left Uncle Cliff with Dad for a bit."

"This is very irregular," the battleaxe said, repeating her earlier comment. Her insistence on obeying the rules was starting to get on my nerves.

The older man, who bore a pretty good resemblance to Tom, seemed confused by the exchange, as well he might.

"I told you I wasn't happy about that man being allowed access to—"

"Hi, Granddad," Sam said, interrupting the sister. "Dad's…He looks pale and…" His lip trembled.

I scooted my chair closer and gave Sam a one-armed hug.

"Hi, Mr Jenkinson, I'm Mark and this is my partner Simon. We're friends of Tom and Cliff," Mark said, standing and taking the man's hand. Then he turned to who I assumed was Tom's mum. "Pleased to meet you, though I wish it were under better circumstances."

Feeling Sam had regained control, I also stood and shook hands with the Jenkinsons.

"I'm sorry, but I will have to ask the man who is with your son to leave. Like I said, we only allow immediate family outside visiting hours," the sister broke in.

Tom's dad turned to her. "Cliff is family."

"Yes, but I mean—"

"He's Tom's husband, domestic partner, lover, whatever you want to call it."

"Yes but—"

"But nothing." Mr Jenkinson drew himself up to his full height; if anything he was an inch or so taller than his son. "My son's partner will not be dictated to by a Nazi in a blue frock".

"I should call security," she persisted, though I could tell she was weakening.

"All I want is to see my son," Mrs Jenkinson said, looking as though she was about to burst into tears at any second. She'd remained virtually silent until this point, so her comment seemed to focus everyone's attention.

"I'll take you in now, Grandma," Sam said, getting up and leading her away.

"I'm not happy about all of this." Obviously the sister still had some fight left in her. I had to give her points for tenacity, if not humanity.

"I don't give a fig if you're happy, sad, or turning cartwheels down the middle of the ward. My son needs his family around him at a time like this, and Cliff is the most important member of his family."

The sister let out a long breath, threw up her hands and walked away.

"I used to eat characters like her for breakfast when I was in the army," he told us once she was out of earshot. "And it's the first time I've heard anything about being a grandfather." He smiled.

We explained who Sam was.

"So he's the famous Sam, is he? Tom never stopped talking about him when he came back from Spain last year."

I chuckled.

"If you'll excuse me, I'll go and see what our Tom has gotten himself into."

"TOM'S DAD'S JUST like Tom," Sam said in awe.

With Tom's family by his bedside, Mark, Sam, and I decided to go in search of a visitor's canteen.

"He had that sister's number, that's for sure," Mark said, buttering a slice of toast.

"Somehow I can't see the old bag doing cartwheels up and down the ward," I said trying to picture it.

"Huh?" Sam said after swallowing a bite of his bacon sandwich.

We explained what Tom's dad had told the sister while Sam was taking his grandma to Tom's room.

Sam beamed. "I wish I'd heard it. I bet that nurse was

pissed, uh, upset."

Mark shook his head, smiling. "And what about you. All this 'I want to see my dad now' business?"

"It just popped into my head."

"The bit about not thinking you'd need identification was brilliant," I said, mussing up his hair.

"I was on a roll by then."

We ate the rest of our breakfast and then went for a walk around the hospital grounds. We followed a footpath that took us past various flower beds that looked pretty forlorn but I imagined would be a riot of colour in the warmer months. Wooden benches were provided at regular intervals, but it was too cold to sit out that day. There was even a pond with a fountain, but the latter wasn't running.

After we'd been out for about an hour, my nose and ears were really feeling the cold so I asked the others if they wanted to head back.

I was surprised by the number of people in the corridors smoking. Some of the people had dressing gowns on, obviously patients sneaking out for a quick smoke. What was most surprising though was the large number of doctors and nurses who were also puffing away.

We climbed the stairs to the next level and made our way back to Tom's ward.

Mr Jenkinson was sitting in the waiting room when we arrived.

"Any news?" I asked.

"He's more awake and is talking a little."

Sam asked, "Can I go see him?"

Mr Jenkinson nodded.

Before Sam left I told him not to stay long, Tom was weak and would need to rest.

It seemed the sister from hell was on her break, so we felt we could breathe more easily.

❖

A SHORT WHILE later Mrs Jenkinson came out to us. She tried a weak smile. "Why don't one of you go in and see him? He's still a bit groggy, but he's asking after you."

"You go first," Mark told me.

"Okay, thanks."

Cliff was still sitting in the same chair, still holding his man's hand when I entered.

"Hi," I said quietly.

"Simon," Tom said from behind his oxygen mask. His voice was croaky from the anaesthetic.

"How you doing?" I asked.

"Been better, though it'll take a lot more than a couple of young thugs to keep a good postie down."

Cliff sniffed. "They nearly killed you."

"Rubbish, if they hadn't gotten me by surprise, they wouldn't have stood a chance."

"Tom, you heard what that doctor said, an inch lower, and, and…" Cliff shook his head.

I went over to Cliff and gave him a hug. "He'll be back to normal before you know it."

Cliff blew his nose. "It's just the blade went so near his main artery…"

"I know." Turning to Tom, I asked, "Do you know why they…why you were attacked?"

"Giros." Tom said, referring to the money orders the government mailed out to the unemployed and others claiming short-term benefits.

Seeing Tom was tiring, I leaned over the bed and squeezed his hand. "I'll go now. But you behave yourself, okay? Make sure you do everything the nurses and doctors tell you to."

Tom smiled and nodded. "Thanks for coming, but you shouldn't have. All this fuss."

"You're worth it. And I couldn't stop any of them from coming. You try saying 'no' to Sam."

I left Tom's room and went back to the waiting room. A

few minutes later Mark went in, leaving Sam and me with Tom's parents.

"You met Tom and Cliff when they were on their last holiday, didn't you?"

"Yes, Mrs Jenkinson."

"Please call me Iris, and my husband is Ralph."

I nodded. "We were on the same floor of an apartment complex."

"They said they had a great time with you three," Ralph put in.

"We did with them."

We exchanged details about our various families, what we all did for a living, that kind of thing.

The sister passed with a couple of men dressed in suits.

A minute later, Mark and Cliff came up the corridor. It seemed the men with the sister were policemen, and they wanted to interview Tom.

Cliff turned to Mark, Sam, and myself. "It was good of you to come, I don't know what I'd have done without you."

"That's what friends are for," Mark told him, and I nodded my agreement.

"Thanks. I don't think much else will happen today, so rather than waiting around here, you might as well go home."

"You sure? We don't mind staying if we can be of any more help," I said.

"I'm sure." Cliff rubbed the back of his neck. He looked tired. "Once the police have left I'm hoping Tom will go to sleep."

"Looks like you need a nap yourself," Mark observed.

Cliff sighed. "I feel like I've aged ten years today, and it isn't even lunchtime."

I patted him on the back. Then I asked, "What about your car?"

Cliff explained to Ralph and Iris about how he couldn't get the car started that morning. It turned out Ralph knew his way around a car's engine and offered to have a look at it.

With a promise from Cliff to phone us later in the day with an update, Mark, Sam, and I said our goodbyes and left for home.

Chapter 12

SAFELY BEHIND OUR front door, Mark took me into his arms. "Probably shouldn't admit this, but the first thing I thought about when I knew what had happened to Tom was, thank God it wasn't you."

I nodded. The same thought had occurred to me about Mark. "Tom's safe, we're safe."

Mark backed me up against the front door and started to kiss me. Naturally, I gave as good as I got. My kisses migrated from Mark's lips to the right side of his face, and then to his ear.

"Love you," I whispered.

"Love you, too." Mark let out a moan when I slid my tongue into his ear. "You'll have me coming in my pants if you carry on doing that."

I cupped Mark's groin. "Is that a gun in your pocket, Mr Smith, or are you pleased to see me?"

Someone knocked on the door.

"Damn. Just when things were getting interesting," I said, moving away from the door and turning round to face it.

"Mr Peters?" a bruiser of a man said, looking between me and a clipboard. Given his denim overalls, I doubted he was a Jehovah's Witness.

"Yes?" Maybe I could get rid of him quickly.

"We've got a shed for you. Sorry we couldn't deliver it this morning. Truck got a puncture."

"That's all right." I'd completely forgotten about the shed coming. I looked at Mark, silently telling him to take over.

"I'll show you round the back." Mark went out through the front door and disappeared round the side of the house.

A second—equally as beefy—guy got out of the lorry and followed clipboard guy.

After retrieving the cheque and invoice from the Bateses, I put the kettle on and hailed the shed crew from the back door. I knew full well the best way to get good service from a workman was to offer frequent refreshments.

The two men—who introduced themselves as Roger and Eric—took me up on the offer.

I waved a packet of chocolate chip cookies at them.

"Oh, ta," Roger said.

Mark gave me a stern look which I pretended not to see, thus not acknowledging I was giving away his precious biscuits.

ONCE DONE, THE shed looked really good. The light was beginning to fail by this point in the afternoon. Mark and I went to investigate once the men had packed up their tools and driven away.

"Now where were we?" Mark asked, pinning me in a corner

of the shed.

"My mum warned me about men like you, accosting innocent people, dragging them off into dark places and having their
wicked way with them."

"And she was dead right to warn you," Mark said before
crushing his lips to mine and grinding his crotch against me.
"Ah, still hard I see?"

"Of course." I grinned. "I thought those workmen were
really hot the way they used their big hammers to pound in
those nails."

"I've got a big nail I'm going to pound into you," Mark
growled, doing the crotch grinding thing again.

"Oh, that *is* a big nail."

He nibbled on my earlobe. "And it's all for you."

This always turned my knees to jelly. If Mark ever wanted
something, and I was putting up a fight—as if I'd deny him anything—all he had to do was start biting on my left ear, and he
got his way instantly.

"Where's the stuff?" he asked, licking around the shell of
my ear.

I shuddered. "Surely you don't want to do it in here?"

He bit down.

"Ahh! They're, uh…" I couldn't be expected to think
clearly with his nibbling my ear like that.

"Where." He blew warm air into my ear.

"I, uh. Behind the left scatter cushion on the sofa. I'll get them."

With great reluctance I disengaged from Mark and, promising to be back in less than a minute, ran into the house.

We'd made love in every room, not that there were many.
So it came as little surprise Mark wanted to do it in the shed,
too. Turning over the cushion, I came up empty. I looked behind the other cushion, still nothing. Same for the armchair.

"Damn!" I wondered if Sam and Billy had taken them.

I raced upstairs where I knew we had a supply in both bedside tables.

"Eureka!" I snatched up a full tube of KY and stuck a couple of condoms in my pocket.

Rushing back downstairs, I was just about to leave through the back door when the phone rang.

"Bugger!"

Going back into the front room I picked up the phone. "Hello?"

"Hi, Simon, You sound out of breath." It was Cliff.

"Uh, yeah." I felt my face heat. "How's Tom?"

Mark, no doubt wondering where I'd got to, came in and stood next to me. I held the receiver so we could both hear.

"He's still weak of course, but doing better. Although he's complaining of pain from the wound."

"Oh dear," I said.

"The doctor gave him something just before we left."

"Uh huh?"

"Are Tom's parents staying with you tonight?" Mark asked.

"Oh, hi, Mark. Yeah, they're staying until Sunday."

"Good," he said.

"The injection made Tom sleepy, so we decided to come home."

"Sleep's the best thing for him," I said.

Cliff agreed.

We spoke for a few more minutes, but Cliff was sounding tired, and Mark and I had a shed to christen, so, feeling a little guilty, I didn't prolong the conversation. Cliff promised he'd call if he needed anything and to keep us updated. So we said our goodbyes and I hung up.

"Thank God he'll be all right," I told Mark.

"Yeah." Mark nuzzled the back of my neck.

"You still up for it then?" I asked, reaching behind me and feeling Mark's rapidly growing bulge.

"Always." He started licking my neck. This sent shivers down my spine.

"Still want to do it in the shed?"

"Yeah." He was rubbing my bottom now.

I turned to face him and licked his lips. "You sex-crazed beast."

He smiled. "Your sex-crazed beast."

I laughed.

"I should throw you over my shoulder and carry you back to the cave, uh, shed, so I can breed you."

"That would put your shoulder out. And I've seen enough of hospitals for today."

Mark took my hand and we started for the shed. We'd just reached the back door when we heard Sam coming in through the front.

"How's a guy supposed to get a decent fuck when it's like Piccadilly Circus round here?" Mark groaned, dropping my hand and turning around.

"We're in the kitchen," I called out, chuckling.

Sam came into the kitchen and took one look at us. "What's got into you two?"

"Nothing," I said, trying to look innocent.

"Yeah, right," Sam said.

Obviously my poker face needed work.

"Why're you here anyway?" Mark asked. "We've only just gotten rid, uh, said goodbye to you."

Sam rolled his eyes. "Mum wanted to know if you wanted to have dinner with us tonight."

"It's okay, we've, uh, made other arrangements," I said, trying not to squirm. Mark was cupping and squeezing my arse.

"Right, I'll tell her you're about to shag each other silly then," Sam said, turning to leave.

"Don't you bloody dare!" Mark said, catching up with him and tickling him.

After Sam had settled down again, I asked what time Helen was planning to dish up.

"In about half an hour I think."

"We'll be there," Mark said. "Thank your mother for us."

"I will," Sam said, closing the front door.

"Quick." Mark took my hand and led me outside. "Let's get to that bloody shed before anyone else interrupts,"

"It's totally dark now," I said, stumbling my way along the path.

"So? You know where everything is, don't you?"

"I think I can remember."

The darkness was even more complete inside the shed with the door closed. I turned around, found my target and pulled down Mark's zipper.

"I can always find this," I said, putting my hand inside his trousers and giving his equipment a light squeeze.

"C'mere." Mark wrapped his arms around me.

"Shit!" I said.

"What?"

"I left the condoms and lube in the kitchen."

"Oh for fuck's sake!" Mark said. "You stay here, and I'll go and get them. Don't you dare move a bloody muscle."

He left, and I waited where I was told. We'd have to do it standing up, with me bracing my hands against one of the shed walls. There was no way I was going to get down on that hard floor.

"Okay, found them." I then heard the crunch of gravel as he came up the path. A couple of seconds later I heard a crash, followed by, "Fuck!"

"Mark? You okay?"

"Who the bloody hell left that rake there?"

I left the shed and almost fell over Mark, who was on all fours on the ground.

"You all right?" I asked, trying not to laugh.

"Yeah. Don't think I've broken anything."

I helped him up and started to lead him back to the house.

"No." He stopped walking. "I'm going to shag you in that bloody shed if it's the last thing I do."

"You smooth-talking romantic, you," I simpered.

"Shut up and get back in there and pull your trousers off."

"You've got such a wonderful line in foreplay." I helped him back to the shed and closed the door behind us.

I took off my trousers as ordered and felt around for a hook to hang them on.

"What's wrong now?" Mark was starting to sound exasperated.

"Where can I put my trousers?"

"Just throw them on the floor."

I reluctantly complied, putting my underpants with them, too.

I waved my arm around until I found Mark. "It's gone soft," I said, grasping his limp dick.

"What did you expect with all this palaver?"

But it wasn't long before I'd got him hard again.

I don't know if it was the thought of having sex in the virtual outdoors, or the possibility—albeit remote—of discovery, but Mark really did turn into a sex-crazed beast.

Of course his initial stretching was as gentle as ever, if a little more hurried, but once he was fully seated and had assured himself I was comfortable, he definitely let me have it.

I didn't know if it was the frustration of being interrupted, or the innate need to breed after near tragedy, but Mark went at my prostate with abandon. I loved every second.

"Need you," Mark panted, thrusting me against the shed wall.

"You got me." I pushed my arse into his pistoning hips.

"So tight," He grunted.

"So big."

Marks hand found my straining dick and pumped it a few times.

"I'm close," I warned, wanting us to come as close together as we could.

"Me, too." Mark bit down on the side of my neck. I screamed and squirted into the inky darkness.

Behind me, Mark's body went rigid as he fired his own load into the rubber.

"Oh, God," he groaned.

I silently agreed, seeing angels and other glowing heavenly beings float across my vision.

We leant against the shed wall, spent from our exertions. Slowly I became aware of my surroundings, the smell of newly sawn wood mixed with some kind of chemical wood preservative.

My teeth started to chatter.

Mark tightened his hold on me. "Cold?"

"Yeah."

I didn't think the temperatures could have dropped that much while we'd been fucking. Scrabbling around in the dark, I searched for my trousers and underpants.

"You need to install a light in here," I said, hitting my head against the door.

"No electricity," Mark said from next to me. He must also be looking for my clothes.

"Well, a battery light or something."

"Ah, here we are." Locating my outstretched hand, Mark put my trousers into it.

"Are my underpants somewhere there, too?"

"Hang on." He fumbled around a bit more. "Yeah, here you go."

I started to dress. "Yuck!"

"What?"

"I must have squirted my cum on my trousers, it's all down the front."

"THERE'S ONE THING," I said, coming down the stairs a few minutes later, wearing a change of clothes.

"What's that?"

"We know our new shed is able to withstand pretty rough treatment."

Mark handed me my coat. "Maybe you should write them a letter, telling them their sheds are able to withstand the mating of sex-crazed beasts."

"My sex-crazed beast." I touched his cheek.

Chapter 13

"VISITORS!" TOM EXCLAIMED from his hospital bed, his large bulk propped up by several pillows.

"Hello," I said, approaching the bed and giving him a kiss on the cheek.

Tom's colour had improved since the last time I'd seen him. Also, he was free of the tubes and the oxygen mask had been removed.

"You look a lot perkier," Sam said. We'd had to bring him along, of course. As Billy was planning to spend the weekend with Sam, we'd brought Billy, too.

Cliff had phoned me the day before and asked, if we hadn't anything else on, to pay Tom a visit. Virtually being confined to bed was making Tom bored and irritable. Cliff hoped some fresh faces would brighten his mood. It seemed to be doing the trick.

"What's the food like?" Billy asked timidly. I could see he was in awe of Tom's size.

"Bloody awful!"

"Tom!" Cliff admonished, gesturing to Sam and Billy.

Sam smirked and Billy giggled. I knew they'd heard much worse.

The conversation moved on to the ward sister from hell and how Tom teased her by being super-nice, smiling, and waving at her.

"I bet that winds up the old bag no end," Mark said.

"Why do you think I do it?" Tom chuckled. "Oh, ah, ah!" He clutched at his chest, his face showing how much pain he was in.

Cliff stood and reached for the nurse call button.

"I'm all right," Tom said through clenched teeth. "It only hurts when I laugh."

Cliff sat, but I could tell he was ready to leap up again should Tom so much as twitch.

We were distracted by the clatter of the lunch trolley coming down the ward.

"Did you order vegetarian, Mr Jenkinson?" the orderly asked, coming into the room.

"Depends." Tom eyed the man suspiciously.

"On what?"

"On whether the veggie option is more edible than the carnivorous one."

Sam sniggered.

The orderly went to his trolley and came back with a tray which he placed on Tom's over-the-bed table.

Tom looked at his food with contempt. "How am I supposed to get well eating that muck?"

"Sorry, Mr Jenkinson. That's all there is."

"Do you eat this food, too?"

The man looked down at the limp salad, curling and dried

sandwiches, and bowl of watery soup. He shook his head. "God, no."

We laughed, which brought on another grimace from Tom.

"That's it, I'm going to get the nurse to give you some more pain pills," Cliff said, brooking no argument. He left the room.

"He does fuss," Tom said, breathing heavily.

"And you'd be up the proverbial creek without a paddle if it wasn't for him," I said.

Tom nodded, the pain easing from his face.

Cliff returned with a pleasant-looking woman in a sister's uniform. She must have been the weekend cover for the battle-axe in blue.

"Your partner tells me you're having a wee bit of pain." The sister's wonderfully soft Scots accent alone would have acted as an analgesic for me.

"Cliff's overreacting."

Cliff shook his head. "He's had at least three pain episodes this afternoon. Each time it was when he laughed."

The sister held Tom's wrist and looked at her pocket watch.

"And I'm just talking about a chuckle, not a full-on laugh," Cliff continued.

"I'm fine," Tom assured.

Cliff let out a breath and shook his head.

The sister let go of Tom's wrist and noted something on the chart at the end of his bed. "Your pulse is a little high." She then examined the dressing on Tom's chest. "Are you in pain now?"

"Be honest," Cliff told him.

"The odd twinge, but I can live with it."

"The doctor wrote out a prescription for pain relief should you need it. And I think you need it."

"Thank you, Sister," Cliff said.

"Okay," Tom sighed.

Dosed up, Tom steadily began to doze. "I'm sorry, he said after one particularly wide yawn.

"We'll leave you for a bit while I show the others around

York," Cliff told him. "Then they can pop back in to say good-bye before they go home." Cliff looked over at us to see if we were agreeable.

"Works for us," Mark said.

"If you take my car, there should be enough room for the five of you," Tom said.

Cliff kissed his man on the forehead. "I'll bring you a little something back from that deli by the Minster."

"Make it a big something," Tom said sleepily.

TOM'S DAD HADN'T been able to fix Cliff's car, so it had been towed to a repair garage. Fortunately a couple of Tom's work-mates had driven Tom's car from the sorting office, so Cliff wasn't without transport.

Cliff told us the local council didn't encourage cars in the city centre, so they'd set up various park and ride schemes. Within ten minutes Cliff pulled into one of the park and ride collection points and told us a shuttle bus would take us the rest of the way.

"Can we go to the National Railway Museum?" Billy asked.

"Would you mind waiting till we're with Tom?" Cliff asked. "He likes taking people there."

Billy smiled his agreement.

"So, what do you recommend we look at?" I asked.

"I'd like to show you the Minster, if you're interested."

"That sounds great," Sam said. "We went with the school, but that was ages ago."

Cliff consulted his watch. "There shouldn't be a service at the moment, so we'll go there now."

Once the bus dropped us off, we walked round the ancient city, slowly making our way through the cobbled streets to the huge, but oddly not imposing Minster.

"Cor! These streets are narrow," Sam said at one point.

"If you look up, you can see how the upper storeys of the

buildings stick out," Cliff said. "From the top storey you could almost hold hands with someone in the building opposite."

"Oh, yeah," Billy said, looking up."

We entered the Minster through the Great West Door.

Cliff motioned for us to come closer. Speaking quietly, he said, "Officially, this place is called the Cathedral and Metropolitical Church of St Peter of York, though that's a bit of a mouthful, so everyone just calls it York Minster."

"Why is it called Minster when it's a cathedral?" Billy asked.

"Minster means that it has a staff of clerics in its own right. Although like you said, it's also a cathedral."

"York's a city because it has a cathedral, like Ripon and Wakefield, right?" Sam asked.

Cliff nodded.

We began to explore the cavernous interior. But despite the Minster's size, I felt an amazing sense of intimacy; it was hard to explain.

In the middle of the nave Sam tilted his head up to the vaulted ceiling. "How tall is it?"

"Not sure," Cliff admitted.

I didn't think Cliff was often caught out like that. I remembered him being a mine of information when we were in Menorca.

"I know that at its highest point, the Minster is one-hundred-and-ninety six feet." Cliff smiled, no doubt glad he could at least provide one relevant fact.

As we walked around, Cliff went on to tell us a little of the Minster's history. It seemed there'd been a place of worship on the site since the 7th century, though the current building wasn't started until 1220.

"Of course, it's still being built, or at least maintained."

"I remember seeing television pictures of the burning roof," I said. Years earlier a fire had destroyed the roof of the south transept.

"Yes." Cliff sighed. "So much damage, and it's still being repaired."

We looked at the famous Rose Window which was being renovated.

"It was lucky to survive the fire," Cliff said. "Fortunately they'd had the window re-leaded a few years before, so although the glass cracked into thousands of pieces, it all held together."

The window was beautiful—in fact, they all were.

"But it's so light in here. You'd have thought with the size of the building it'd be dark," Mark said.

Cliff nodded. "And most of the glass is original."

At one point while the others were investigating one of the side chapels, I took a moment to sit in a pew to enjoy a couple of minutes of quiet reflection. I realised how lucky I was. Less than a year ago I was drifting through life seemingly without purpose. Then along came Mark, my strengthened relationship with Sam, and Sam's newfound relationship with Billy. Finally there was a new friendship with Tom and Cliff. I was a lucky man to know all these people. After giving thanks for such blessings, I offered up a prayer for Tom's rapid recovery.

"WASN'T JORVIK THE old name for York?" Mark asked Cliff as we made our way toward the museum of that name.

"The Viking name, yes. The Anglo-Saxons called it *Eoforwic*, and before that the Romans called it *Eboracum*."

Cliff was a history teacher. I knew he was in his element with four eager students to educate.

"I don't think this place was here when I last came," I said after paying the entry fee.

"It opened in April 1984. I was here on opening day," Cliff said, blushing a little.

We sat in what Cliff called a time car. It was a car-like vehicle that moved on a track. At first the car travelled backwards, showing us various aspects of British life starting from the present and going back in time using images of the Second World

War, the nineteenth century, all the way back to the Viking age.

Then the car changed direction and drove forward through a Viking village. Through various life-size models, sounds and smells, we were able to get a somewhat realistic glimpse into what life must have been like back in the tenth century.

The boys found the smell of the Viking drains particularly interesting. Cliff told us later they recreated the various odours by heating scented oils. I didn't ask how they knew what Viking drains smelled like; I wasn't sure I wanted to know.

ON SEEING US, Tom rubbed his hands together. "What did you get me?"

"And good afternoon to you, too," Cliff said, entering Tom's room ahead of the rest of us. "I had a great time showing the boys round the Minster and the Jorvic museum."

"Sorry, I'm glad you had a good time, but I'm hungry. You saw what my lunch was like."

Billy chuckled. "The food where my Gran lives is like that."

"Has she complained?" Tom asked.

"Nah, but then she's got Alzheimer's."

"This food'll send me round the bend if I have to eat it much longer," Tom grumped.

Cliff shook his head. "We can't have that." He opened his shopping bag and produced a number of brown paper bags which he arranged on Tom's table.

"No." Cliff smacked Tom's hand. "That's Mark's, and the one next to it is Sam's." He indicated which bags were Tom's.

After the museum we'd called in at a deli, the place surpassing the one I used at home. There'd been a bewildering choice of breads, pastries, pies, cakes, and tarts. Cliff had asked us what we wanted and refused to allow us to pay for anything, telling us it was his way of saying thank you for the help we'd given him earlier in the week. The amount of food Cliff had bought for Tom would have kept me fed for at least two days, but Cliff had assured me Tom would wolf it down and be hungry again by suppertime.

Tom tore into his many paper bags, exclaiming over and tasting the contents of each.

"It's like feeding time at the zoo," Cliff whispered to me.

I smiled and nodded, delighted to see Tom getting back to his old ways.

Chapter 14

"GRAN, WE BOUGHT loads of decorations last year," I told the determined pensioner as she fought her way through the other shoppers at the outdoor Christmas market.

Gran had "invited" Mark and me to do some Christmas shopping with her. As there was no way to ever refuse her invitations, the first weekend in December had seen us driving over to Leeds.

"You might see something you like."

I doubted it, but Gran was on a mission, and there was no convincing her otherwise.

"Reminds me of when Mary took us shopping last year,"

Mark said, trying to keep Gran in sight. It would be all too easy to get separated in the crush of bodies.

"Tell me about it," I said, narrowly missing being run over by a fleet of pushchairs being driven in Panzer formation between two stalls, barely allowing anyone to pass in the opposite direction.

Many of the decorations on sale were dreadful and cheap-looking; I wouldn't give them houseroom. Mark spotted some electric candles he said would look nice in the front window. So we got a couple of sets of those. I hoped that would satisfy Gran, it at least would show her that we'd made an effort. But no.

"That artificial tree looks really natural." She pointed.

"It's at least eight foot tall!" I protested, imagining the thing taking up the entire living room.

"The ceilings at home are about ten feet tall, aren't they?" Mark asked.

"We'd have nowhere to store it for the other eleven months of the year."

"That builder provided storage space at the sides of the loft conversion, didn't he?" Gran asked.

Gran had given us the money for Paul Bates to convert our loft into a second bedroom. Occasionally she slept there, but mostly it was used by Sam and Billy when their parents allowed them to spend nights at our house.

"We don't need a big tree." My arguments were getting weaker, but I wasn't giving up just yet.

Mark turned on his pleading puppy-dog eyes.

"Stop it! If we got that tree it would need so many lights we'd have to ring the electricity board every time we wanted to turn them on." Yes, I was exaggerating, but even so.

"Bah, humbug. You're no fun today," he pouted.

Was I being a Scrooge? Hoping we could reach a compromise, I caught the stallholder's attention and asked her if she had a smaller version of the tree. She did, but even I had to admit it didn't look nearly as impressive as the full-size one.

"We'd have to get a lot more decorations," I argued. Even

though we'd bought plenty last year, I knew they wouldn't be enough for a tree that size.

"True." Mark rubbed his hands, clearly getting into the Christmas spirit.

"How would we get it home?" Yes, I was weakening.

"Don't you have a roof rack?" Gran asked, her eyes twinkling.

I was definitely being ganged up on.

"Okay, I give in."

Mark launched himself at me. And, despite being in the middle of a crowded market, he laid a big wet kiss on my lips. I took a look around but apart from a couple of surprised glances, no one said anything.

"We should get it last, I'm not lugging something that size around all day," I said, trying to be practical in the face of emotion.

We must have visited every stall—Mark examining the merchandise, asking questions of the stallholders—before either agreeing to buy something or pointing out that a different stall had the same item for a cheaper price. I was proud of my man; if he kept it up he could become a naturalised Yorkshireman.

"I notice you haven't bought much," I said to Gran later in the morning.

"Oh, no, I've got all the decorations I need."

I stared at her. "So why on Earth are we here?"

"When I spoke to Mark the other week he happened to mention that you two needed more decorations."

My stare switched to Mark.

"Well." He looked down at his trainers that were toeing at the concrete. "I said we could maybe use a few more things, not..." He widened his bag-laden arms. "I never thought the Christmas market would be this big."

I continued to stare.

"I thought it'd be fun and I like Christmas shopping and..."

In the more than a year that I'd known Mark, this was the first time I could ever truly say I was angry with him. I felt deceived...lied to. Mark knew how much I hated crowds, he also knew how much we'd spent on repairing the boiler, the new shed, and Sam's birthday present. Okay, I could rationalise that he hadn't intended on buying a huge Christmas tree, but even so, he must have known what a Christmas market was like.

"Simon?" Mark asked at my continued silence.

I turned away from him, tears stinging at my eyes. I hated myself for showing such weakness, and in front of Gran, too.

"Simon?" It was Gran's turn. She was just as bad—egging Mark on, joining him in his scheme. "Don't go there."

I looked up at her. "And just where should I go?" I tried to keep my voice even, but it wasn't easy.

"I'm sorry," Mark said. "I just thought it'd be fun Christmassy, and…" He dried up at my withering glare. "We don't have to get that tree, it is a bit expensive."

"And what would we put all this stuff on?" I asked, lifting up the several bags of decorations I was holding. Mark and Gran were similarly burdened.

"They might agree to take them back?" Mark offered.

Closing my eyes, I took several deep breaths. I hated being angry and upset—hated even more that it was at Mark, the man I loved more than anyone else.

"Come on, let's see if we can find a café or something," Gran said, nudging my shoulder.

The crowds were getting thicker and I was sick of having people bump into me or step on my feet. I was pretty mad at the world in general, and maybe a cup of coffee would help.

Thanks to Gran, we managed to get the last table at a coffee stall. It was still outside, so there was no opportunity to get warm, but the coffee was hot enough.

The walk to the coffee stall had been silent, which gave me an opportunity to see things more rationally. I knew Mark had had a pretty shitty set of Christmases once his mother died. I suspected the last one when she was pretty ill hadn't been that much fun either. So I could understand why he wanted to make the most of the holiday now.

"Simon," Mark started once he'd taken a drink of coffee.

"It's okay. I'm sorry for snapping at you like that. I know you got carried away with what we bought…we all did."

"It did get pretty crazy. But I'm sorry that I got you here under false pretences."

I smiled, though I suspect quite weakly. "It's okay. I know I need a kick up the arse now and again. I'm a stick-in-the-mud and…" I knew I had a tendency to overdo the Yorkshire thriftiness.

"You're not a stick-in-the-mud," Gran said.

I shook my head. "We both know I am. You were right to get me to come here. Despite the crowds, I have to admit I've had a fun morning."

"I wouldn't have you any other way," Mark said, taking my hand under the table. "And I'm sorry."

"I'm sorry, too." Leaning closer I said, "We can show each other just how sorry we are tonight at home." We'd planned on spending the night at Gran's, but I wanted to get my man home and have lots of make-up sex in our own bed.

Mark's radiant smile told me he understood and agreed with my plan.

"Well, thank goodness that's over with," Gran said, draining her mug of tea. "Walking across the market with two men with faces like a wet weekend wasn't how I wanted to spend the day."

Mark and I grinned at each other then at Gran

"Now you two have kissed and made up—"

"We haven't kissed," I told her.

Mark soon rectified that, much to the shocked displeasure of a woman with two young kids at the next table.

"As I was saying," Gran continued. "Now you two have kissed and made up, it's time to buy that tree, then we can get out of here."

Mark looked at me, his expression carefully schooled into neutrality. I knew he was waiting for me to decide.

"Sounds like a plan."

Out came Mark's thousand-watt smile.

When we pushed our way back to the stall, there were only a handful of the large artificial trees left. Gran went into full barter mode and got a few quid knocked off the price. I don't think telling the woman that we were doing her a favour by taking one of the last trees off her hands so she could go home and put her feet up cut much ice, but nevertheless, Mark and I were soon proud owners of an eight-foot Naturalook Norway Spruce.

"I'M TELLING YOU, it's not going to go in," I said in frustration.

"Maybe if we try it at a different angle."

"It's too big!" I grunted. "Maybe if we squash the sides."

"It would get stuck, and then where would we be?"

I sighed. "We've tried every way possible." I refused to get angry, not twice in one day.

"Sorry. It seemed a good idea at the time, and I really wanted—"

"I know." Getting an idea, I said, "Let's take the tree in first, then collapse the box and leave it out for the dustmen. There's no way we can keep the box in the storage space next to the boys' room. If it won't go through the front door, it certainly won't fit through that small opening in the loft."

Mark nodded and went into the house for a kitchen knife.

"What you got there?" Sam asked, coming into the front yard with a grinning Billy in tow.

"A tree," I said.

"You could fit a forest in there," Billy chuckled.

"It's big enough to house a third world family," Sam added.

I'd had much the same thoughts when we'd battled to fasten the enormous box to the roof rack. It had taken all my knot-tying skills to make sure the thing wouldn't come loose during the journey home.

Once Mark had cut into the box and exposed the contents, Sam gasped. "How big is it?"

"None of your business," Mark grinned.

"I meant the tree." Sam giggled.

"Eight feet," I told him.

"What are you going to do with the old tree?" Billy asked.

"I thought we could put it at the top of the stairs," Mark said.

"Your house will look like a fairy grotto by the time you've finished," Billy said.

"They are a couple of—"

"If you want to live to see your sixteenth birthday next week, I wouldn't continue down that road if I were you," Mark said, lifting a section of the main trunk out of the box and threatening Sam with it.

"Sorry," Sam said, repressing a giggle.

The boys helped carry in the sections of the tree, laying them out on the living room floor.

Mark proposed erecting the tree there and then as it would be pointless taking everything upstairs only to have to bring it back down again in a week or so.

I smiled to myself, knowing he'd suggest something like that. "Okay, good idea." Looking around at all the pieces, I asked, "Where's the assembly instructions?"

Mark went outside, saying he'd collapse the box and look for them. He came back a couple of minutes later, a frown on his handsome face. "They're in Chinese."

Sam chuckled.

"Isn't there an English translation?" I asked.

Mark turned the sheet over. "No."

Sam's chuckle turned into a laugh.

We spent over fifteen minutes trying to attach one bit of tree to another, and still the thing looked more like a badly-cut hedge than a Norway spruce.

"This is hopeless!" Mark eventually conceded, dropping two pieces of branch that refused to connect.

"Maybe we should take the sheet round to the Chinese takeaway for them to translate," Billy suggested.

"I'll go and get dad," Sam said.

"Why, does he read Chinese?" Mark asked.

"No, but he's good with his hands. Or at least that's what Mum always says," Sam said as he and Billy left.

Within ten minutes of Paul's arrival we had our tree built.

"That's amazing," I said. "Thank you."

"No problem." Paul nodded, rightly proud of his achievement.

"HAPPY BIRTHDAY!"

"Thanks," Sam said, smiling up at me from the kitchen table.

Paul and Helen had agreed to allow Mark and me to buy Sam a portable colour TV for his bedroom. At first they'd protested that it was too much, but we'd convinced them he was worth it.

Unfortunately, Mark was working late and was forced to miss Sam's party. However, he'd promised to take Sam and Billy to York to see Tom and Cliff at the weekend.

"It's a telly!" he said after tearing off the wrapping paper.

"Uh, actually, no," I said, keeping a straight face. "It's a sack of potatoes that I emptied into a television box. The telly itself is in Mark's and my bedroom."

Sam shook his head, knowing I was pulling his leg. "Thank you. I've been after Mum and Dad to get me one for ages."

"You're welcome."

Apart from his parents, I was the oldest person there. As always, Helen put on a great spread. After eating a few sandwiches and enjoying a slice of his birthday cake, I made my excuses and left the teenagers to it.

HEARING A KEY turn in the lock, I put down my book and watched as my exhausted partner came through the door.

"Rough day?" I asked, standing and giving him a hug.

"No, just long," He yawned.

Daphne had decided to stay open late to serve meals and light snacks to the Christmas shoppers. The longer hours meant Mark was often exhausted when he came home, but he was able to console himself with the overtime pay and the extra tips.

"Want a bath?"

"Please," he said, nodding.

I followed him upstairs, helped him undress then went into the bathroom to start the water running. When I returned to the bedroom, I found Mark fast asleep.

AS PROMISED, WE'D taken the boys to Tom and Cliff's Saturday evening, telling them they'd have to spend the night on an inflatable mattress in Tom and Cliff's front room. That hadn't put them off in the least.

Tom had been discharged from hospital about a month earlier and was railing against the restrictions the doctor's had placed upon him. Cliff had hoped, like the hospital visit, that we'd be a distraction for him.

"Wow, these're expensive. You shouldn't have! But thank you," Sam said, opening Tom and Cliff's present.

After talking with Paul and Helen, Tom and Cliff had decided to get Sam a video games console.

"We thought it would go with your new telly," Tom said, receiving a hug from the excited teen.

"It's ace! Thank you."

"Can we try this on your TV?" Sam asked, picking up the console.

"'Course you can," Cliff said, getting up and going round the back of their set to disconnect the coaxial cable. "We know it works because the big kid over there insisted on road-testing the thing as soon as we got it home."

Tom grinned. "We couldn't give him a faulty gift, could we?"

"Did it take three afternoons playing the space invader game to determine that it was working properly?"

"It's addictive," Tom defended.

Cliff just smiled.

Sam and Billy played games for a while, but our stomachs began to rumble, so we soon adjourned to the kitchen.

We ate a delicious meal which was rounded off with another birthday cake—a chocolate one this time.

Once Sam and Billy had helped clean up the kitchen, we returned to the front room for an impromptu video games tournament, "teens against oldies," as Sam termed it.

Needless to say, the teens won; however, one-on-ones between Sam and Tom were more closely fought and very competitive.

"IT'S TIME FOR us oldies to go to bed," Tom said, after Sam had beaten him at tennis.

Mark and I needed an early night, too—Mark more than me with his long work days. We helped the boys set up the air mattress, Cliff providing sheets, a quilt, and a couple of pillows.

With a request to the boys to keep the noise down if they chose to play on the games console, us four oldies climbed the stairs to bed.

"I NEVER KNEW it was so big in here," Sam said.

After breakfast, Tom had asked the boys what they wanted to do. Billy had repeated his wish to visit the National Railway Museum, and everyone was in favour. To my surprise there was no admission fee, but visitors were asked to give a donation, something I was more than happy to do.

The boys had moved over to some of the steam engines on display.

"Coppernob!" Tom read the nameplate aloud to the giggling boys.

"It's called that because the raised portion above the boiler is made of copper," Cliff told us.

"Look, you can get your fingers inside," Billy said, exploring a tear in the smooth copper cladding.

"The holes were made by flying shrapnel when the station where Coppernob spent the war was bombed," Cliff told us.

"Can we see the Mallard?" Sam asked.

We walked over to the famous locomotive.

I read the information board, which told me the Mallard held the record for speed by a steam engine. It reached one-hundred-and-twenty-six miles-per-hour.

Sam, who was reading the panel with me said, "Even the trains of today don't go that fast."

"The record's a bit misleading," Cliff said. "The speed was achieved while Mallard was pulling a test train, it wasn't fully laden, and it only reached that speed for a quarter of a mile going downhill."

"It knackered up the cylinders, didn't it?" Tom asked.

Cliff nodded.

Clearly the men knew their railway history.

The boys loved how they and Tom could climb on the footplates of many of the locos. I wasn't sure who was having the better time, Tom or the two boys.

"This clock," Cliff said, pausing our group by a particular exhibit, "used to be at Euston station in London. Clocks were very important to the railways. Any idea why?"

I smiled; Cliff was a born teacher.

"They'd want the trains to run on time, I guess," Billy said.

"Yes, that's part of it. But before the railways, people took their time from a local source. The Town Hall clock or whatever. Some people used sundials, like the one we have in our garden, but these are difficult to use, and of course the sun has to be shining."

Sam nodded.

"Back then, every town had its own local time. It didn't really matter if, say, the time in Leeds was different from the time in York. But when the railways came, accurate and standardised time throughout the country was needed."

We were beginning to attract a crowd; Cliff's interesting and easy-to-understand delivery was proving to be a magnet.

"The time in a town on the West coast of Britain could be as much as half an hour earlier than the time somewhere on the East coast. When you wanted to catch a train, at say, five minutes past eight in the morning, you didn't know if that would be five past eight local time, or the time calculated from the place where the train had begun its journey."

Billy asked, "You mean, if it took an hour for a train to get from Leeds to York, and it set off from Leeds at five past seven their time, it would arrive in York at five past eight Leeds time, but that might not be five past eight York time?"

"Exactly." Cliff smiled. "So, to make things less complicated, many railway companies decided to take their time from Greenwich in London.

"The time in Leeds, for example, was six minutes and ten seconds earlier than at Greenwich. As the railways became more important in daily life, gradually everyone began to use the time from Greenwich, or 'railway time,'" Cliff sketched air quotes, "for everything."

"Was the six minutes and ten seconds difference because the sun rises that much earlier in Leeds because it's further west than Greenwich?" I asked.

"Yes, you've got the idea."

"WHAT'S SO INTERESTING about a wooden box with loads of

lead shot in it?" Sam asked as he walked over to another exhibit.

Sam had been full of questions all morning, and Cliff had been more than happy to answer them. Unlike at the Minster, Cliff hadn't been stumped once.

"Ah, that's from the 1855 great train robbery."

"The one with Ronnie Biggs?" Billy asked.

Cliff shook his head. "No, that was a different, and more recent, train robbery."

"Oh," Billy said.

"Like I said, it was 1855, and Britain often sent quantities of gold over to Europe to pay for various things. William Pierce and Edward Agar knew this, and over the months and years cooked up a plan to steal some of it.

"The gold was loaded on a train at London Bridge station, taken off at Folkestone and shipped across the channel to France. Obviously it was well-guarded...in fact it was put in wooden crates," Cliff pointed to the exhibit, "which were locked into safes that needed a couple of keys to open them. Agar was able to get hold of these keys for short periods and made wax impressions of them."

We were starting to attract another crowd.

"The gold weighed about two hundred pounds, and if they'd have just put the empty crates back into the safes, then once the boxes were weighed, they wouldn't have been heavy enough, and the crime would've been discovered. So they arranged for carpetbags of lead shot to be left in the guard's van. They moved some of this lead into the boxes en route to Folkestone, where they left the train."

"That's clever," Sam said.

"Very. Although the weights didn't correspond exactly when the boxes were weighed at Boulogne, they were still allowed to travel on. When the boxes were opened in Paris, the lead shot was discovered.

"The French said the crime must have happened in Britain, and the British said it happened in France. It would probably have remained unsolved if it wasn't for a woman called Fanny Kay."

Cliff had his audience totally now.

"Fanny was, or used to be, Agar's girlfriend. Agar was awaiting transportation to Australia after being found guilty of a different crime—one he probably didn't commit. He wrote to Fanny, mentioning that Pierce was supposed to have given her about seven thousand pounds—a fortune back then—but Fanny said she hadn't received a penny. She roiled up an investigation by trying to question Pierce—already in prison on another charge—and Agar testified against Pierce and the other co-conspirators, one of whom was the guard on the train."

"Wow," the boys exclaimed.

Cliff promised to lend me a book on the subject that went into more detail. I liked reading about true crime, but confessed I hadn't come across this one before.

We moved over to look at some rather nice first-class carriages. The Victorians sure knew how to travel in style. However, a quick glance over at Tom showed us that the big guy was tiring but doing his best to hide it.

"I'll take you home," Cliff said, "and the others can drive back in their car once they've had enough."

"No, it's okay, I'll just go sit in the car. You come out when you're ready, but take your time."

"It wouldn't be the same without you," Sam said. "We can come back again another time, when you're stronger."

Tom ruffled Sam's hair. "Thanks, little mate."

"WE'VE VISITED YOU a couple of times now," Mark said, giving first Cliff then Tom a hug.

We were outside Tom and Cliff's house later that day, about to leave for home. I wished it could have been a longer visit, but what with Tom still convalescing and Mark's long hours at work, it was all we could manage.

I picked up Mark's thread. "So it's about time you came over to see us."

"Okay," Cliff said.

Cliff looked at Tom, and they did their own silent communication.

Once they'd come to an unspoken agreement, Tom turned to us. "Are you doing anything at New Year?"

"We hadn't planned anything. Sam's Uncle Steve is coming down from Scotland during Christmas, and he's staying in our spare room, but he's going back home for Hogmanay. So you're welcome to stop a couple of days or whatever around New Year," I said.

"No. I'm giving my bed to Uncle Steve and I'm staying with you," Sam told us.

"First I've heard of it," Mark said.

"Well, you've got a double bed up there," he persisted.

"Ah, and you'll be wanting to share it with Billy, I suppose," Tom said with a grin.

"Absolutely." Sam replied, not batting an eyelid.

"Well, why don't we come on Wednesday, the thirtieth, and stay until Friday, New Year's Day?" Cliff suggested.

"I think we'll have kicked the boys out of the room by then," Mark said.

"Charming!" Sam said, not hiding his sarcasm.

"It's a date then," Tom said, rubbing his hands together.

"Please don't expect any spectacular scenery like this," I said, sweeping my arm across the rural panorama.

"It'll be fine," Cliff assured us.

Just then it started to spit with rain, so we all said our goodbyes and wishes for a happy Christmas.

"And thanks again for my games console," Sam said, giving Cliff a hug and Tom a gentle squeeze before getting into the backseat next to Billy.

"You're welcome," Cliff said.

"See you after Christmas," Tom called out as Mark reversed down their driveway.

Chapter 15

"YOU AWAKE?"

No," Mark mumbled, his voice thick with sleep.

Ignoring him, I said, "I just realised something. It's a year ago today that you came to live with me."

"Oh yeah," he said, sounding more awake. "Want to do anything special?"

"You remember the meal I cooked for you that night?"

"Chicken and pasta?"

I was thrilled he'd remembered. "I want to cook it again. Would that be all right?"

"No, I want to cook it, and I want to feed it to you this time."

When Mark had first moved in, his hands were bandaged and I'd had to do almost everything for him, including feeding him.

ONCE WE'D CLEARED away the breakfast dishes, we walked into town to buy our joint Christmas gift to each other. After seeing, and hearing, Tom and Cliff's CD player, we'd decided to get one and hook it up to the stereo in the front room. By the late 1980s more and more music was becoming available on compact disc, and the sound section of the library was starting to build up a reasonable collection.

"This is a very popular model," the sales assistant said, pointing to a particular player.

I got out the measuring tape I'd remembered to bring with us. "Sorry, it's twenty millimetres narrower than the rest of our system."

The sales assistant probably thought I was being picky, but as the whole thing had to stack, I wanted it to match. I knew I didn't have to buy the same brand for the CD player as the rest of the system, but it would have to look similar to the other components.

"This is the size you need." He tapped on the front of another player.

"Can we give it a listen?" Mark asked.

The man frowned. "It isn't wired up."

After an uncomfortable silence where I expected the guy to offer to connect it to an amplifier, I asked, "Could you connect it? I'm sure you don't expect people to buy products without hearing them first."

"If you don't like it when you get it home you could always bring it back."

Knowing there were a couple of other hi-fi retailers in town, I silently communicated to Mark that we were leaving.

"Okay, thanks, we'll think about it."

Our reception in another shop was much better. The place was busy, but the sales assistant treated us warmly and took his time showing us the various models that were available. He even asked us if we'd brought along our own CD to listen to. I'd borrowed a disc of classical highlights just for this very purpose. The man said we'd be better off listening through headphones, as this would cut out much of the background noise from the shop. Another good idea. He put in the disc, pressed play, and my ears were filled with glorious sound. After a couple of minutes I took off the headphones and gave them to Mark to try. He listened for a while then nodded his approval.

We tried a couple of more machines that fitted the style and colour we wanted before making our choice.

Once we'd got the CD player home, I asked, "Are we going to wrap it and not open it until Christmas Day?"

"Might as well. We've only got the one disc."

I'd planned to get Mark a few country CDs to open on the day.

For their main gift, we'd bought Sam and Billy a set of walkie-talkies. This, we reasoned, would save their parents a fortune on phone bills. I'd checked that the distance between their respective houses was within the range of the equipment. It was, though we'd have to warn the boys anyone could tune into their frequency, and so they'd have to be careful what they said over the air.

"I'LL START DINNER," Mark said, looking over at the mantel clock.

"I'll come and sit on the stool, just like you did a year ago."

"Are we being silly?" he asked.

"Probably, but I don't care."

I sat myself down on the stool as promised and gazed at the awesome man I loved more than anyone else in the world preparing our meal. I marvelled at his grace of movement; none of his actions seemed unnecessary; when he reached over for a knife, it was there; he didn't have to scrabble around to find it.

Mark put all the food onto the one plate, though I recalled the first time I fed him, I'd used two; but this minor detail was of no importance. After that first meal, we'd decided putting all the food on one plate was easier.

"Open wide for the choo-choo train." He'd remembered my words of a year ago. I couldn't help the huge grin on my face.

It was great fun, if a little messy, being fed by Mark. I had to sit on my hands at one point, because it's a natural human reaction to want to reach out and feed oneself. I began to appreciate a little of how frustrating life must have been for Mark back then. I voiced these thoughts to him.

"I remember feeling my arms begin to move, but you always seemed to know what I needed. It was weird, but in a really good way."

"It was my love for you. I felt a deep connection to you right from the start."

He took me in his arms. "Love you."

"Love you, too," I said, returning both hug and kiss.

"Hi, only us!" Sam said, letting himself and Billy in through the front door. "You two at it again?" he asked, appearing in the kitchen doorway.

"Sod off!" Mark said.

Sam just beamed at him.

We explained how we were recreating our first meal together. Admitting it to someone else made it sound stupid and mushy and…

"Awesome!" Billy said and Sam nodded his agreement.

"You two glad to be out of school for the holidays?" Mark asked.

"Yeah, but we've got loads of homework," Billy put in.

"I'm not surprised. It's your exam year after all," I said, immediately knowing I was sounding like a librarian. "Have you eaten?" Now I was coming across like a mother.

"At mine, but…" Billy started to explain.

"I'll see what we've got." Mark stood.

By all accounts Mrs Tranter was a terrible cook, so Billy was often hungry when he visited.

❖

A FEW WEEKS earlier I'd been given directions to a local farm that had turkeys for sale. Mark and I went one weekend to check the place out.

We knocked on the farmhouse door; a plump woman in her sixties—every inch the typical farmer's wife—answered. We explained that we wanted a turkey about ten pounds in weight, and asked her if she could accommodate our needs.

"Of course, my dears," she said, wiping her hands on her apron. "Come with me."

She led us to one of the outbuildings at the other end of the farmyard. I could hear the noise of turkeys getting ever-louder as we neared a particularly large and rundown barn. She ushered us inside and closed the door behind us. The noise, smell, and chaos inside were indescribable.

She shouted above the din. "Do you want to pick one out?"

Suddenly the idea of serving a nut cutlet on Christmas Day began to have a strong appeal.

"Don't forget they've still got some growing to do," she told us.

"It's okay, just give us one you think will be best," Mark said, going a bit green around the gills.

The woman laughed. She knew what she had done, damn her. After stepping out of the barn, I took several deep breaths.

"They'll be plucked and ready for collection the Wednesday before Christmas."

We agreed on a price and she wrote down my name and the size of bird we wanted. Then, and not a moment too soon, we hightailed it back to the car.

So it was with more than a little trepidation I drove back to the farm that Wednesday. I was on my own, as Mark was still working.

After queuing for a short while outside the farmhouse door, I gave my name, handed over the money, and took delivery of a large cardboard box, a few strands of straw poking out the top.

The box went in the boot and I drove home, relieved not to have come face-to-face with my Christmas dinner.

As I had the previous Christmas, I'd bought way more food than we'd ever eat, but you never knew.

Sam and Billy told us they were going to try and eat at three different houses on Christmas Day. They were having the starter with Mark and me. I'd bought a whole salmon that Mark said he would poach. They'd then go down the street to Sam's house for the main meal, and then it was across town to Billy's place for Christmas pud.

It was vital therefore that the three meals be co-ordinated to a strict schedule. Though Mark and I had been invited to share the whole meal with the Bateses, there would be Paul, Helen, Steve, Sam, and Billy, plus Paul's parents, and baby Charlotte of course. Mark and I thought Helen had enough on her plate without us as well. Mark had been planning the meal for weeks, so he was glad we'd chosen to eat at home. This was another of his ideas for paying me back for the meal I'd cooked the previous year. I told him it wasn't necessary. He agreed, but said he wanted to do it anyway. How could I refuse?

CHRISTMAS EVE ARRIVED at last. As Mark had to work for the first part of the day, I decided I'd work the half-day, too. Though frankly, there was little for me to do. Many of the librarians had booked the day off, so I'd offered to act as cover if I were needed, but few readers came through the doors. So I spent most of the morning in my office doing some much-needed filing.

Once the clock had dragged its way round to half twelve, I locked the front doors and exchanged Christmas wishes with the staff before letting them out. After doing one final check, I, too, left.

Mark was just putting his coat on when I got to the café.

There were a few diners just finishing their meals, but Daphne said she'd deal with them.

AFTER A LIGHT lunch, I went upstairs to wrap a few more presents. I'd wondered about getting something for Tom and Cliff. Eventually Mark and I had decided to get them a watercolour of the Yorkshire Dales that we'd seen in an antiques shop. I didn't recognise the artist, but the shopkeeper assured me she was local. Rather than trusting the postal service, we'd decided to hand over the gift when Tom and Cliff came to visit. Me being me, I'd worried that our friends would be embarrassed if they didn't have anything to give us. Mark had smiled, told me not to worry, and called Tom and Cliff to explain what we'd decided. Turned out, Cliff had had the same idea about waiting until the thirtieth, and Cliff—like me—was worrying about possible embarrassment if the gift exchange was one-sided.

After Mark had told me that back when he was small, his mother had allowed him to open a gift on Christmas Eve, I'd suggested we should revive the tradition. That had earned me several kisses and, ultimately, a sore arse.

I began to separately wrap the plush rabbit and pig we'd bought for baby Charlotte. She'd been born early on the twenty-seventh of December. I felt a little sorry for Sam and his sister. Their birthdays being so close to Christmas, they'd often just receive the one present.

Finished, I carried the wrapped gifts downstairs and set them under the tree.

"All those for me?" Mark asked.

I threw one of Charlotte's gifts at him. "I'm sure you'll enjoy receiving a furry pink pig."

"Oh, just what I always wanted!" Mark started to tear at the paper.

"Mark!"

He grinned and told me he'd rewrap it later.

I swayed my hips as I walked over to him. "I do have a special present for you."

"Can we unwrap it now?" He rubbed the front of my trousers, which were beginning to tent.

I nodded toward the stairs.

Before chasing me upstairs, Mark dead-bolted the door. "To stop any possible teenage interruptions," he explained.

In the bedroom Mark pulled down my trousers and underpants in one move. Then he burst out laughing. "And you say I'm kinky."

Before going downstairs with the gifts I'd tied a large red ribbon around the base of my dick.

"You like?" I asked.

Mark licked his lips and showed me just how much he did like.

A little while later, still cuddled around Mark, I heard a car door close, and Sam's excited voice float up from the street. Getting up, I peeked through the bedroom curtains.

"Steve?" Mark asked.

"Think so."

We both went down the street to greet him.

"You must be Mark!" The man held a hand out to me. "And this good-looking man must be Simon!"

"No, Uncle Steve, it's the other way round." Sam giggled.

"Sorry. I plead travel fatigue."

"You haven't driven all the way in one go, have you?" Helen asked.

"I stopped off at a service station about halfway for a cup of coffee and a sandwich."

"That's good," she replied. "Though I imagine you could use another cup by now?"

"Please."

We all trooped into the Bates's kitchen. Walking behind Steve I was able to get a good look at him. He was in his mid-to-late-thirties, about five feet ten inches, and had brown hair that was turning grey at the temples.

"Did you bring me a present, Uncle Steve?"

"Sam!" Helen said.

"Sure did. Two, in fact. One for your birthday, and another you'll have to wait till tomorrow to open."

Sam beamed.

Helen just shook her head. "There's been a change in sleeping arrangements." She explained the situation to her brother.

"No problem." Turning to Sam, Steve asked, "And where's this famous Billy I've heard so much about?"

"At his house. He's coming over later with some clothes so he can stop for the odd night."

"Where's he sleep when he comes over?" Steve asked.

"With me," Sam admitted shyly.

Steve raised an eyebrow.

"So long as they behave, Paul and I don't mind," Helen said, offering her brother a biscuit.

"Wow, Sis, you are liberated. God knows you didn't get it from Mum and Dad." He took a digestive and dunked it in his coffee.

"No," Helen said.

"How are they?" Steve asked, though I could tell he found the subject painful to talk about.

"No idea, we haven't seen them since May Day."

"When they turned on Sam?"

Helen nodded.

"Shit, will they ever learn?" Steve said with bitterness.

Sam was becoming uncomfortable; the rejection by his grandparents still hurt.

"Do you want to get your stuff over to ours, then your uncle will have more room to unpack?" Mark asked.

"Thanks. I'll be back soon, Unc."

STARING INTO THE fire later that evening, I told Mark, "We'll burn that Yule log tomorrow."

We sat and held hands, gazing into the leaping flames.

Mark eventually broke the silence. "I haven't told you much about what life was like for me at home, have I?"

"Not really."

"I've always thought all this was a safe zone, you know?" He gestured to our modest living room. "It's a place where I feel comfortable, at peace with the world, somewhere where no bad things can happen to me. It all stems from when you'd have me round when…"

"I know," I said softly, not wanting to say out loud that he felt safe here when I'd purchased an hour or two of his time.

"And I could forget for a couple of hours everything that was going on outside."

I kissed his cheek, silently giving him my support.

"So, I guess what I'm saying is, I feel safe letting things out when I'm here with you." Mark took a few deep breaths and continued to stare into the fire. "I used to try so hard to get Dad to like me. When I was a small boy, I'd come home all excited from school holding a picture I'd drawn in art class, or a model I'd made in woodwork, that kind of thing. When I was a little older I'd show him a medal I'd won at sports day or a good grade I'd received for an essay I'd written. But the most I ever got out of him was 'Oh, that's nice. Now run along and show your mum.'

"He never did the usual father and son things with me like taking me to the swimming baths, playing football or cricket in the back yard, or taking me fishing with him, even though I'd begged him to. He always said I'd get under his feet."

I ached to say something, to offer some words of reassurance, but I knew he had to let go of this without interruption.

"I remember once in English, we were asked to write a piece entitled 'My Dad'. The teacher said if we didn't have a dad, we could choose someone else to write about. Do you know…I couldn't find anything to say. I just stared at that blank page for ages. I think it was at that moment I gave up trying to please him.

"The last Christmas Mum was alive, she tried to make the best of it for me. She'd made a nice dinner and everything, but she wasn't feeling well, the cancer had already gotten hold of her, so she didn't eat much. Looking back, it makes my heart ache to think of the effort she made to make the day a good one for me."

I nodded.

"The last Christmas I spent with Dad was pretty bleak. The only thing that made it different from any other day was that dad was drunk earlier than normal.

"I'd made a dinner for us both, but I bet he didn't say more than two words throughout the meal. As soon as it was over, he crashed in front of the telly, I cleaned up, and he didn't help of course. 'Woman's work,' he called it. So once I'd washed the pots, I went round to a friend's house and tried to soak up some of their Christmas cheer. Though as I've told you before, I didn't really have any close friends, so I felt uncomfortable about butting in at such a close family time."

I rubbed his arm, my heart breaking for the bleak past he'd had to put up with. Although I wasn't overly close to my parents, they'd provided me with a safe and stable home, and although we didn't often say it, I knew they loved me.

"I don't know why I bothered, but I'd bought him a Christmas present, I think it was some aftershave and a bottle of talc. I didn't earn that much money." Mark sighed. His voice remained flat and emotionless. "He didn't even bother opening it."

I'm not a violent person by nature, but by God, if Mark's dad had been in the room then, I swear I'd have clonked the bastard over the head with the poker. I tried to contain my anger, but Mark must have spotted it.

"He isn't worth it. Don't get yourself worked up, he just isn't worth the effort."

I don't know who was comforting whom. We just held each other. I didn't have the words to tell Mark how much I ached inside for his plight. I don't think I needed to, Mark instinctively knew. Our unspoken connection was in full operation.

A key turned in the lock, shortly followed by, "Only us."

"Hi, Sam," I said, still holding onto Mark. "Did you two have a good time with Steve?"

"Yeah, he's been telling us stories about all the blood and gore he has to work with. Did you know he has hammers and chisels just like Mr B?" Billy always called Paul Mr B.

"I think they'd be a little different," I said. "They'd have to be an awful lot cleaner, too."

Steve was an orthopaedic surgeon.

"Oh, yeah. We did asepsis at school," Billy said.

"You all right, Mark?" Sam asked, looking directly into Mark's face.

Mark sighed. "Just reliving a few memories of when I still lived at home. But here with Simon, you, and Billy, things couldn't be better."

"Oh, right. That's good." I could tell Sam felt awkward.

Mark nodded, smiled, and seemed to pull himself together. Looking over at the clock, he asked, "Do you all fancy going to church for the midnight service?"

"Uh, yeah, why not?" Billy said.

I smiled, remembering the service we'd attended the previous year. In fact, I was ashamed to realise it was the last time we'd been to church.

"Is it raining?" I asked.

"No, but it's cold, and the wind's starting to get up," Billy said.

"Do you want to walk it? It isn't that far to St John's."

AFTER SUPPER, WE wrapped up and went to church via the Bates' house to tell them where we were going.

"I'll tag along, if you don't mind," Steve said.

"Sure. The more the merrier," Mark said.

Paul also decided to join us, too. Helen stayed at home to look after Charlotte.

"I might even see if I can get some sleep," Helen said. "Because no doubt you'll be coming round here early to open your presents," she said to a grinning Sam.

"Of course. Set your alarm for five o'clock, Mum."

"I'm putting the dead bolt on the front door then." She ruffled her son's hair.

We all made our way to the church. Conversation was lively; Steve had a ready wit. He told us a few funny stories about the pranks he and his fellow students pulled when they were at medical school. Many of these seemed to have a bedpan involved in them somehow. The man could have made a brilliant after-dinner speaker.

DESPITE THE HEATING being on in the church, I could barely sense any rise in temperature from the outdoors.

Billy was in the lead and found us an empty pew about halfway down the aisle. Mark followed him in. Sam squeezed himself in next. I gave him a look, but of course this didn't faze Sam in the least. So I sat next to the teenager, Steve was next, and Paul, our token straight, sat at the end.

The organ played quietly in the background as the church filled. I bowed my head and spent a few moments collecting my thoughts, thanking the Almighty for shining his love on me and the people around me. I prayed for Mark's father, hoping someday he'd come to realise what a truly wonderful gift he'd thrown away.

The service began with a lone boy soprano singing the first verse of "Once in Royal David's City." A tingle ran up my spine at the clarity of the choirboy's bell-like voice. The choir joined in for the second verse, and the whole congregation sang the remainder of the carol.

The service was similar to last year. In his sermon, the vicar stressed the importance of family togetherness at Christmas.

During the carols, Mark's beautiful voice could be discerned above those of us who possessed a less stable set of vocal chords. Billy hadn't heard Mark sing before, so he frequently glanced over in awe.

It was fantastic to be able to hug each other during the celebration of the peace. I remembered feeling a little self-conscious the previous year, but I had no such qualms this time around. And I had to admit Steve had a nice set of muscles on him.

As with the previous year, the service concluded with my favourite carol, "Hark! The Herald Angels Sing."

During the walk home, I felt brave enough to hold Mark's hand. A brief glance behind showed Sam and Billy doing the same.

"Hey, Dad, why don't you hold Uncle Steve's hand?" Sam piped up.

To my, and I'm sure Steve's, amazement, Paul actually did take Steve's hand for a brief while. Paul was so comfortable with his sexuality he could hold another man's hand without batting an eyelid.

Chapter 16

"HAPPY?" MARK ASKED.

We were holding hands on the sofa. Sam and Billy were sitting on the floor in front of the blazing fire, unwrapping their presents. I was the happiest I could remember, with the possible exception of this time the previous year when Mark told me he loved me.

"Doesn't seem like a year ago," I sighed.

"I know." Mark squeezed my hand.

"Walkie-talkies!" Billy said. "Wow!"

"Cool!" Sam said. Turning to us, he added, "Thanks."

"You're welcome," Mark and I both said simultaneously.

The boys then opened all their other gifts, which were mostly practical.

"Great, I needed a new pair of these," Billy said, taking the lid off a box of trainers.

"Your dad told us you did," I said.

"Come on you two, open your presents from us," Sam said, placing wrapped parcels into our hands.

"You shouldn't have. You don't get that much pocket money," I told them.

"Of course we should," Billy insisted.

They'd gotten us a couple of CDs of romantic classical music. "So you two can snuggle up together and be like an old married couple," Sam said, rolling his eyes.

"Thanks," Mark said.

"And what's wrong with being like an old married couple?" I asked.

The boys giggled.

They'd also gotten Mark a box of his favourite sweet biscuits, and I received a book on Victorian philanthropy.

MARK GOT ON with the dinner, refusing to allow me to help.

Just before one, the boys returned, full of news about what gifts they'd received at Sam's house.

"Come and sit down," I told the boys. "First we're going to pull the crackers. So take off your right shoe and sock."

Naturally this confused them.

"Last year, because of my bandaged hands, I couldn't pull my cracker," Mark explained. "So Simon took off my shoe and sock, and I pulled my cracker using my toes."

"And we wanted to keep the tradition alive," I said, feeling foolish once again. It had seemed like a good idea at the time.

The boys giggled but did as they were asked.

Then Mark got the salmon from the fridge and everyone tucked in.

"Delicious," I told the chef, who smiled.

Sam wanted seconds but I told him that, with everything else he was going to eat, he should pace himself.

The boys soon left to go eat their main course. Mark then brought out the turkey and all the trimmings for us.

I TUNED TO the Christmas afternoon movie. They were showing *The Sound of Music* again. As there was little else on, and neither of us had seen the film for a few years, we collapsed onto the couch and began to watch. I must have fallen asleep at some point because the next thing I was aware of was Mark getting off the sofa. It was dark and he was drawing the curtains.

After turning on the tree lights, he asked, "Didn't you say something the other day about a Yule log?"

"Yeah. I put it just inside the shed."

Mark went out but came back almost immediately, cradling something in his arms.

"What's that?" I stood to get a better look. "A kitten?"

The tiny thing was mostly black with white sock markings on the bottoms of each paw. The lower half of its face was also white.

"Where did you find him? I'm assuming he's a him?"

"Oh, yes, there's no doubt he's a him." Mark smiled. "He was outside the back door."

I ran a fingertip along the kitten's back. "He's so small and thin." The poor thing must have only been a couple of months old. He was shivering.

Mark began to make baby-talk type noises to the kitten.

"I wonder if he eats turkey? God knows, we've got enough of the stuff," I said.

Mark handed the kitten to me and went into the kitchen; I followed, holding the now sleeping ball of fluff.

"If I mince up a bit of the meat and add a drop of gravy, that should be all right I think," Mark said, getting the meal together.

"Do you think he'd like a saucer of milk, too?"

Mark smiled. "We'd have to dilute it with some tap water. Cow's milk has too much lactose in it."

I stared at my partner; he was a font of information.

"The woman who lived down our street took in strays," Mark explained.

The kitten took a little of the food, but really liked the diluted milk.

"Aw, isn't he cute?" Mark said, lying on the floor next to the cat. Looking up, he asked the question I'd been expecting. "Can we keep him?"

"He probably belongs to someone else." Although thin, the kitten seemed well cared for.

"Do any of our neighbours have a cat?"

"There's Mrs Potter at the end of the road, but she's got a tom, so it won't have been born there and got lost."

"I want to keep him." Mark turned on his pleading expression.

As if I could ever refuse him when he gave me that face and, anyway, I liked the little cat, too. "Okay. But if someone else claims him, you'll have to give him back."

Mark got up off the floor and hugged me.

Returning to practical matters, I asked, "Are you going to get that log, because it'll still be burning on Boxing Day if you don't put it on the fire soon."

"Sure. Do you think Tiddles will want to go out for a pee?"

"We're not calling him that!"

"Nah, we'll have to think of something."

The cat didn't want to go back out. Can't say I blamed him; it was really cold outside and the wind had gotten up again. So Mark went out alone and retrieved the Yule log.

Within half an hour we were on the sofa, Tiddles—that name would have to go—stretched out on the hearth rug in front of the crackling fire.

"Hi. Only us." The teenage invasion was back on.

Out of the corner of my eye I saw a black blur run into the kitchen.

"What was that?" Sam asked.

Mark got up and went into the kitchen, returning a moment later, the kitten in his arms.

"Oh," Billy said. "Where did you find him?"

"He kind of found us. He was outside the back door about an hour ago," Mark explained.

"He's cute. What's his name?" Sam asked, stroking the kitten's head with a fingertip.

The kitten started to purr.

"Well, I thought about—"

"No." I interrupted. "We're not calling him Tiddles."

The boys laughed.

Mark sat back on the sofa and the kitten curled up on his lap.

Various names were batted around, many of them seasonal. However, Santa, Chris, and Yule just didn't fit.

Then Sam suggested Noel.

"Noel…Noel. I like it," Mark said, turning to me.

I shrugged; it sounded good to me.

"Noel it is." Mark rubbed the kitten's ears.

Noel sat up at the sound of his new name, so we concluded he agreed with our choice.

I reached over, took one of Noel's oh-so-tiny paws into the crook of my finger and said, "Welcome to the Smith-Peters home, little Noel."

He gave a tiny meow, before settling back down on Mark's lap and going to sleep.

"So, what kind of day have you two had?" I asked the boys.

"All right," Billy said.

"You don't sound very enthusiastic about it," Mark observed.

"Things got a bit awkward at mine this afternoon," Billy said, dipping his head.

Sam put an arm around his boyfriend's shoulder and led him to the chair, where they snuggled up together. It was a tight fit.

"Billy's Uncle Bill came round after dinner. He was drunk," Sam explained.

"Ah," I said, understanding beginning to dawn.

"He started saying things to Sam and me about being 'poofs' and 'nancy boys'."

"Oh, no," I said.

"What did your parents say?" Mark asked softly.

"They were great. They told him to shut up or leave," Billy said.

"So what happened then?" I asked.

"He sat in a chair and kept giving us dirty looks. It made me feel uncomfortable, so eventually I took Sam to my room. We could hear raised voices coming from downstairs, but I turned up my stereo, so I don't know what they were saying. When we came downstairs again, Uncle Bill had left. Dad said that he, Uncle Bill, I mean, wouldn't be coming round much anymore."

"I'm sorry you had to face all that at Christmas," Mark said.

"At any time," I added.

Just then Noel meowed, leapt from Mark's lap, and began to squat on the carpet.

"Quick, he's…!" I said.

Sam and Billy laughed as Mark shot off the couch, scooped Noel up, and took him out through the back door.

BILLY HAD BEEN given Trivial Pursuit for Christmas. We divided into teams for a game—Billy and I taking on Mark and Sam. My Sport and Leisure was a bit weak, but Billy knew his sport pretty well, I had Literature and Science and Nature pretty well covered, and Billy and I were about equal on the other subjects. We had a great, but frustrating, time trying to collect the various coloured wedges. We had a few minor disputes concerning the pronunciation of various terms, and whether or not some answers were close enough to the truth to be given, but all in all we enjoyed ourselves.

Mark and Sam narrowly won the game, but I took comfort in the fact they'd had the run of the die.

"Rubbish, we just knew more of the right answers when it came to the wedge questions," Sam declared.

The game took us up to bedtime. We discussed where Noel would sleep, Mark suggesting in the bedroom with us. I nixed that idea straight away, much to Sam and Billy's amusement.

"I suppose you're right," Mark eventually conceded. "I'll wrap a hot water bottle in an old sheet and put it in the box that the CD player came in."

"Good idea. We'll put down plenty of newspaper, to hopefully catch any, uh, little accidents," I said.

Mark agreed. "I'll get a bag of cat litter tomorrow, as well as some kitten food. I think the petrol station should be open."

"What about a litter tray?" I asked.

"The woman down our street used a washing up bowl," Mark said. "I've got that old one in the shed we can use."

"You two are totally smitten with that kitten." Sam giggled at his own pun.

We groaned and told the boys to go to bed.

Mark and I cuddled on the couch, enjoying the peace and quiet until it was time for us to go to bed ourselves.

I went up first while Mark saw to Noel.

When Mark came upstairs, I helped him undress. He could do it on his own of course, but I wanted to recreate a little of what had happened a year earlier. Then I remembered a gift I'd deliberately held back. Reaching into the back of my side of the wardrobe I emerged with a flat wrapped box, which I gave to Mark.

"What's this? And how come it wasn't with the other gifts under the tree?"

"It's private."

Mark's right eyebrow raised. "Kinky private? Something you didn't want the boys to see?"

"Or borrow," I said, anxious for him to open it.

He smirked, tore off the paper, lifted the lid of the box, and burst out laughing. "Oh, my God."

I'd bought, through mail order, a pair of furry handcuffs.

Mark and I had discovered a kinky side to our relationship. I knew this would shock most people who saw me as a buttoned up, conservative, and staid librarian.

"Question is," I said, lifting the handcuffs out of the box and swinging them in front of Mark's face, "Who's going to use them on whom?"

"Do me," Mark said.

I took that to have more than one meaning, but I was up for it, literally.

Mark lay face-up on the bed and I climbed on top of him.

We were face to face, chest to chest, and cock to cock. I began to kiss him all round his handsome face. When his lips were in range he kissed me back. I ran my hands down the sides of Mark's awesome frame, feeling his warmth and the slight fur which covered much of his body. If anything, he was more beautiful than a year earlier. Good food and regular exercise had allowed him to fill out.

Next I glided my hands down Mark's arms, feeling the latent strength in his muscles.

Mark began to touch me in return. He lightly ran his hands down my back, repeating the movement with just a fingertip. This sent electric tingles shooting through my whole body. Cupping my arse cheeks, Mark encouraged me to slide up and down his front.

Our already hard members rubbed together, the leaking pre-cum painting our bellies and further aiding my motions.

We continued to kiss, touch, and caress, but I was getting close and I didn't want to climax this way. Mark needed to be tamed.

Reluctantly I rose to my knees and sat up. Picking up the handcuffs, I dangled them where Mark could see them. "Assume the position, punk!" I really should stop watching so many American cop shows.

Mark smirked but complied. "I'm innocent, Officer Peters."

"Quiet!" Quickly I secured his wrists to the headboard. "Do you have any foreign or sharp objects I should be aware of before I frisk you?"

Mark looked down at his naked body. "First you tell me to be silent, then you ask me questions."

I slapped his thigh for being so insolent.

"Police brutality!" He said, a bit too loudly for comfort.

Staying in character, I told Mark I was about to do a cavity search.

"Shouldn't you read me my rights or something?" Mark protested.

I had to think, not easy with where I was and what I was about to do. "You have the right to remain silent. Anything you say or do can and will be used in a court of law." I couldn't remember the rest of it, my recall not exactly aided by the persistent rubbing of the tip of Mark's dick along my arse crack. "Oh, fuck."

"Yes, please." Mark licked his lips.

I wished I'd remembered to get the lube and condoms out before we'd started—having to break to get them often spoiled the spontaneity—but it was something Mark had been adamant about, right from the start.

Finding the stuff in the bedside drawer, I opened one of the foil packets and rolled a rubber down Mark's dick. He frowned. From his earlier statement it was obvious he was hoping I'd be the top.

Prepare for lift off," I said, squatting over him.

"What show's that from?"

I shook my head, unable to remember. I was trying to juggle so many scenarios, I was bound to lose control of some of them.

I started to lube myself up. Over the past year my arse had gotten used to being stretched, so it didn't take as long to get ready as it used to.

"Ready?" I asked.

Mark licked his lips before nodding.

Raising myself and feeling behind me to line everything up, I slowly impaled myself. The look of bliss on Mark's face as I did so was something to behold. Leaning forward, I captured his lips with mine, and while my insides sorted themselves out, we exchanged soft kisses.

Mark started to thrust up into me, although he wasn't able to get much of a rhythm going. "Simon," he whined.

I smiled, my lips still pressed against his. "You trying to resist arrest, punk?"

"Think I might have a cardiac arrest if you don't start fucking yourself on me soon."

Feeling I'd frustrated him enough, I sat up and took a couple of experimental bounces.

"Yes," Mark hissed.

I wasn't sure how long I could keep this up. Walking to and from work most days helped me stay in reasonable shape, but I'd need much stronger thighs to sustain such activity for any length of time. It was fun to be able to control the speed and intensity of the lovemaking—what had Mark called it, "topping from the bottom?" or maybe it was "bottoming from the top?" But whatever it was, I knew my thighs were about to give out any time.

"Gotta stop," I groaned, rubbing my legs. This was neither erotic or romantic. Maybe we should switch roles, me inside Mark. Lifting myself off, much to Mark's disapproval, I removed his condom and went in search of new ones.

It took a little while longer to loosen Mark up, he was usually the one on top. But once I judged he was ready, I was in there and pumping away, holding Mark's legs in the air.

"You got it!" Mark cried out at one point. I guessed I'd just nudged his prostate, so I aimed for the same spot again.

Deciding to liven things up a little, I started licking the sole of Mark's foot. This made him shudder. Shuddering became full-out shaking when I started nipping at his toes. I knew his feet were ticklish, but I had no idea they were that sensitive.

"Stop it," Mark said, struggling against his bonds.

As I didn't want him to either wake the boys or break the headboard, I reluctantly ceased my foot worship. Although I'd certainly remember that if I wanted to tease him in the future, the mere mention of touching his feet ought to make him putty in my hand.

And speaking of hands, it was about time I wrapped one around Mark's prominent member. The thing had been waving around, dripping a steady stream of pre-cum during our love-making.

I thought about edging Mark then pulling back and letting him cool off again before bringing him back to the brink, but frankly I wanted to get to the finish line just as much as I knew he did. So when his balls rose in their sac I continued to stroke. Several ropes of white semen shot out the end of his dick, flew into the air, and spattered on Mark's perfect flat chest.

I still had a little way to go before my own climax. Mark decided to help me reach my goal by squeezing down with his anal muscles.

"Oh, God," I panted, suddenly getting a whole lot closer than I thought.

Before I knew it I was flying over the edge, collapsing on top of Mark's sweat and come-soaked chest.

Mark found my lips and stole away what little breath I had left. My head swam and my vision blurred, but if I were to die right there and then, then I wouldn't be sorry. But eventually our lips separated and I took in several lungfuls of air.

Somehow, without me knowing, my dick had slipped out of Mark's hole and lay spent on his thigh, the greasy condom slipping off. But rather than deal with it I just wanted to lie there and soak in the love and warmth Mark and I shared, drifting off in post-coital bliss.

"Uh, Simon." Mark rattled the headboard. "Can you release me?"

I lifted my head from Mark's shoulder and looked up at his bound hands. "Sorry." I yawned and rolled off the bed. "Where did you put the key?"

"I never had it."

"Oh." I lifted the box the cuffs had come in, but it was empty.

"Simon?" Mark's voice was starting to rise in pitch.

"It's okay, it'll be here somewhere." I hope, I added silently, visions of having to call the fire brigade out to cut Mark loose swimming through my mind. Then I spotted something small and shiny on the carpet just under the bed. "here we are."

I kneeled up and released my lover, kissing his wrists, which, thanks to the padding, weren't abraded.

"Thanks," Mark said, stretching. "Need the loo." He got to his feet and headed for the door.

"Put some clothes on," I said, remembering the boys were staying with us.

Mark shook his head and opened the door. "I haven't got anything they haven't."

Sighing, I realised he was right. If I could play bondage games with my lover, then I could deal with the idea of a little nudity.

I heard a flush then Mark, still beautifully naked, came walking back into the bedroom, his dick swinging between his legs.

This reminded me, I still had a spent condom to deal with, but where was it?

I eventually found it in a fold of the quilt, and realising I too needed the bathroom, I took it with me.

Back in bed a few minutes later, the lights out, Mark pulled me close. "Been quite a year," he said, kissing me on the lips.

"Best year of my life."

"Mine, too."

Kissing him back, I said, "Happy anniversary."

"Happy Christmas."

About the Author

HAVING READ ALL the decent free fiction on the net Drew could find, he set out to try his hand at writing something himself. Fed up reading about characters who were super-wealthy, impossibly handsome, and incredibly well-endowed, Drew determined to make his characters real and believable.

Drew lives a quiet life in the north of England with his cat. Someday he hopes to meet the kind of man he writes about. Visit him online at drew-hunt.co.uk.

CPSIA information can be obtained at www.ICGtesting.com
Printed in the USA
LVOW072148010113

313907LV00018B/526/P

9 781478 355045